The smell of fear

I could see the dog's great red tongue hanging out, its eyes rolling, hear its baying cries. I reached into my pouch and took Euny's black egg in my hand. Within moments the suffocating smell of the beast seemed to surround us, so that I thought I would choke. I was aware of it crouching to spring, of its huge paw reaching up to drag me from the ledge, of its claws penetrating my cloak and piercing my leg....

JUNIPER

monica furlong

BORZOI SPRINTERS • ALFRED A. KNOPF
NEW YORK

JUNIPER

ONE

1

THE NIGHT I was born, according to my nurse, Erith, was a night of black frost and dense darkness in a bitter January. White owls who lived in some nearby trees never stopped hooting and flying around the palace, or so the story goes. No one slept a wink. Erith thought it was a sign that I was a remarkable child, and by the time I was old enough to hear the story, I liked to believe her. Remarkable or not, I was bathed and oiled and bandaged, as all babies are, and then they dressed me in a little shift and wrapped me in a rabbit skin to keep me warm. My mother and father showed their first baby to the ealdors, the elder statesmen, as was the custom, and then Erith cuddled me all night so that, as she said, I would not feel strange in this new country I had come to.

IN MY EARLIEST MEMORY I was toddling around on the big grassy enclosure at the center of the palace. Many grownups were walking about, men mostly, holding strange forked twigs in their hands. They moved slowly, eyes fixed on the ground, and they did not notice me or talk to me as they usually did. Because I was bored and wanted to copy them, I picked up a forked twig that someone had dropped and began to move toward the middle of the grass. Suddenly I screamed and screamed, so wildly and in such terror that everyone stopped and looked at me. What had happened was that the twig in my hand had turned into a snake. Well, it hadn't really. It was just an old twig, but while I had held it, all of a sudden it had started moving and wriggling in the most horrible way. My father came over to me.

"What happened?" he asked.

"It turned into a snake," I said, knowing that they would all laugh at me because there it was, just being a stick.

"It's all right," he said. "It wasn't really a snake. Would you do it again to show us?"

So rather nervously, but wanting to please, I picked up the twig again by its two handles, and almost at once it began to jerk downward as if it had a life of its own, and once again I dropped it with a yell. I thought my father would be cross with me, but he picked me up in his arms with a laugh.

"Well done, little girl. You've found us another supply of water. We thought there was one here somewhere, but no one could ever find it."

I SUPPOSE I should mention that my father was *regulus*, that is, a small chieftain or king, in Cornwall, and we lived at Castle Dore in the Wooden Palace that he had built on a high grassy place—the site of an ancient fort. There was a house around a courtyard where my mother and father and I lived, a house for the astrologers and another for the bards, an armory, a bakery, quarters for the knights and ealdors, and a big hall where my father dined with them every evening. The house stood in the hills with a long view of farms and other hills, and the air sparkled with that special radiance of Cornish light.

My mother, Erlain, was a tall, graceful woman who was very clever. She could read and write and had learned mathematics and poetry. She could sing beautifully to the harp, and it was she, I heard tell, who brought the bards to our house and with them a very different atmosphere from the days when my father had lived alone with his knights. She taught him to read and write, and gradually, warrior though he was, he began to enjoy learning as much as she did. Later on, as a result, he wanted me to have the sort of good education that girls often do not have even now.

I should tell you that whenever a child was born to a knight or ealdor among my people, the astrologers studied the heavens and its charts to work out the portents for the child's life. Then they wrote some words, almost a sort of poem, to help the child remember the main points, and this was inscribed in tiny writing on parchment and put into a little horn case that was worn on a leather thong around the neck. Later on, when I was older and had learned to read, I liked to take the parchment out and read the words through, just to remind myself. They went like this:

Named for the strong and twisting tree
Of medicine, when she finds the way
By earth, air, water, fire
Then will she mend what is broken.
The dark teacher will correct her,
The fair one will protect her,
The strong man will love her,
And all may be well.

IT DIDN'T make much sense to me because after all, I was *not* named after a tree but was called by the good Cornish name of Ninnoc. The rest of the words seemed just as puzzling.

Other early memories are of a huge chamber at the Wooden Palace with a fire leaping and flickering in the hearth. I had a big bed and Erith had a little one in the corner, but because I felt lonely in my big bed I often jumped out of it and climbed in with Erith. Erith was young and pretty, with red hair and lots of freckles. I used to count them to tease her. Sometimes I woke her to make her tell me a story or sing me one of her Irish songs. I was quite bossy with Erith—I behaved like a little princess who expects the servants to do as she tells them—refusing to get dressed or have a bath or eat my dinner or whatever it was she had to get me to do. Once or twice she threatened to tell my father about my bad behavior, but she never did.

Sometimes my father would appear in my rooms in the evening, just at the time I should have been going to bed, and tell Erith to dress me in my prettiest gown. (I had some beautiful clothes made from pieces of gold and silver material like liquid flame left over from my mother's gowns. I was very proud of myself in them.) I had earrings and bracelets made of silver or set with gems, and on special occasions Erith hung jewels in my long black hair. Erith would put my little squirrel-skin slippers on me and comb my hair, and then I would walk with my father in the procession to the Great Hall. He would sit me on his lap and feed me tidbits from his plate. After dinner I would be passed around on the knees of the knights and they all would tease me and play with me. Once or twice I stood on the table and sang one of the songs my mother or Erith had taught me.

I enjoyed being spoiled, but I was disappointed that my mother did not have another baby who could have been a playmate for me. Only much later did I realize that my parents also wanted more children. But soon I acquired a new playmate whom I will tell you about later, and also Erith let me play with the children of some of the knights and ealdors. We played marvelous games. The old fort on which the palace had been built was surrounded by enormous ditches and ramparts constructed in a maze to make it hard for enemies to find the way in. We raced one another around the ditches, slid down the ramparts on wooden sleds, learned the mazes by heart, and had wonderful games of hide-and-seek there.

Once when we were playing a thin dark-skinned woman approached the entrance to the maze that led to the palace. She had strange black eyes, high color in her cheeks, and a strong, determined gait. She was dressed in worn black clothes, not much better than rags, really, and she did not wear the head covering that all the grown women except beggars wore. Her black hair hung straight down her back, as if she were a child. She wore boots so old that part of her foot showed through one of them. Her whole appearance offended me.

"What do you want here?" I asked bossily.

"I have business with Marcus Cunomorus," she said, sweeping me aside and moving into the maze.

"He won't see you!" I shouted scornfully to her back. After which we children climbed onto the ramparts for the pleasure of seeing her lose her way in the maze. (We had often enjoyed seeing strangers turn repeatedly up the blind alleys until they were forced to ask our help and even to bribe us with a coin.) The thin woman did not lose her way but moved skillfully toward the entrance. The guard must have let her through because a few moments later we could see her making her way toward my father's rooms.

"Who was that woman who came to see you?" I asked him that evening. "The one in dreadful clothes."

"That was Euny," he said, and was silent, although he and my mother exchanged glances. I wanted to ask who she was and what she had come for, but he always discouraged me from asking about things that were not my business, so that I did not quite dare. And that was the last I was to hear of Euny for some time.

IT WAS SOON after this that I found a tiny baby owl out in the fields, and since he appeared to have lost his mother and was in a sad, bedraggled condition, I insisted on taking him home. Erith kept saying that my parents would not allow me to keep him, but I hid him in a small room off my sleeping chamber and only she ever knew. Erith was sure that I would not bother to feed him, but I used to beg mice that the cook had caught in her traps, and other little pieces of meat, and the baby owl seemed quite content. His white feathers looked clean now, especially when he fluffed himself out. I loved to take him on my hand and stare into his blank amber eyes. Sometimes he sat on my shoulder, but often he liked to perch for hours on a shelf over the hearth, dozing in the dim winter light. Later he took little flights around the room, moving beautifully with his wide wings. I called him Moon.

As I grew older, I am sorry to say that I became ruder to Erith. She was often quite worn out from the effort of getting me to rise, wash, and dress, even though it was she who did the work of washing and dressing me. I could never do anything to look after myself in those days. When we went out I was always wanting to go farther than was permitted or to do things that Erith thought were dangerous—walking on the ice of ponds when it was still too thin, jumping over the autumn bonfires that the farm people built at harvest time, climbing high into trees, swinging from one branch to another and refusing to come down. Erith would stand imploring me to do as I was told, torn between her love and care for me and her fear of heights or water or fire. In those days I seemed to be afraid of nothing.

I was tormenting Erith like this one day. I had gone

into the stable where my father's stallion was kept, a great black animal who had lamed a groom and whose kick could probably have killed me. I moved closer and closer to it, determined to stroke it and give it an apple, while Erith, half crying, beseeched me to return to her. I think I knew that I was being stupid, but somehow Erith's pleas drove me on to misbehave.

Suddenly, to my amazement, I felt myself seized by the neck and shoulders and marched out of the stable by someone behind me whom I could not see. As soon as I was able, I turned furiously around and was astonished to see that it was the woman Euny, still as shabby as ever, gazing at me with blazing eyes.

"Juniper!" she said. We stood and stared at each other for a few moments, both of us angry, and then, annoyed that she was rebuking me for distressing Erith, I mumbled, "It's not your business anyway."

Euny did not reply to this but gave me a little push in the direction away from the stable and herself turned and walked off. Glancing at Erith, I saw that she looked sickeningly smug.

"There!" she said. "You've annoyed your godmother."

I was so surprised at this that I forgot about her smug look.

"My godmother! Euny my godmother! Why would someone like Euny be my godmother?"

"That was your mother's choice," she said. "Not that your father disagreed." And she closed her lips very firmly in a way she had when I talked about things that made her uneasy.

So naturally I asked my mother, Erlain, at the first opportunity.

"Is Euny my godmother?"

"Yes."

"Why?"

"Because she is wise. And we needed her."

"Why?"

"I can't tell you now."

"I don't like her. She looks like a beggar woman."

My mother did not answer.

"And she called me Juniper. Why was that?"

My mother laughed with pleasure.

"It was a special name she had for you, your secret name. She whispered it in your ear when you were a baby. Later she told me and said that the secret name was who you really are."

All this seemed very peculiar to me, although not so peculiar as my parents asking this strange woman to be my godmother in the first place. I went out and walked in the ditch between the ramparts to think—a place I often walked when I wanted peace and quiet. There between the grassy walls under a gray spring sky I tried out the name for sound and meaning.

"Juniper. Juniper. Juniper!"

As I spoke it, an extraordinary sense of conviction seized me, as if I had moved and saw the world more clearly and freshly from this new place.

"Juniper!" I said it more loudly, and finally I shouted it as hard as I could.

A sentry's face looked reproachfully over the top of the ramparts.

"Now then!" he said kindly, meaning that making loud noises was worrying to a man whose job was to look out for sudden attacks by our enemies. But I had finished. I knew that Euny, however odd, was right, and that Juniper was my proper name. Later on I had another question for my mother.

"Where does Euny live?"

"She's an Outlander." That meant she lived in the country beyond the farms that were under my father's special protection, in a place where she was always in danger of marauders and brigands.

"Doesn't that frighten her?"

"Not Euny. I don't believe she's ever afraid."

2

THERE WAS only one person at the court whom I disliked, and who I felt disliked me in return—my aunt Meroot. She was my father's older sister. All his life he had loved and admired her, so that when I said I did not like her he would sharply tell me not to be silly. When I was about four, Meroot's husband died in mysterious circumstances. My father had a house built for her in the Wooden Palace, and she and her son, Gamal, who was about my age, came to live with us. Unlike my father, who had wonderful ruddy hair and powerful blue eyes, Meroot had sandy hair and eyes like cold, pale sapphires that I felt watched me critically from behind the curtain of her white lashes. Gamal, on the other hand, was a handsome, blond-haired little boy, not at all like his mother. At once he became a brother to me—we played, slept, and ate together a lot of the time—but as far as we possibly could, we kept out of Meroot's way. Meroot, who my father used to say jokingly would have made a wonderful soldier, was determined that Gamal should grow up strong and fearless, and almost from his infancy she had little suits of armor and small swords made for him and had him trained in fighting and wrestling and archery at an age when most little boys were playing marbles or looking for birds' eggs. She made him wear very few clothes in the winter so that he would become tough (it had the effect of giving him endless colds), and she forced him to sleep on the hard floor with few blankets and to eat the sort of diet soldiers ate. It was a hard life.

Gamal was very loyal to his mother and hardly ever complained, but as a result of these hardships, he spent a lot of time getting warm at the fire in my apartment, wearing a rough coat Erith stitched for him out of a blanket, eating any spare food we had, and occasionally dozing off to sleep in corners. In spite of his mother's treatment he was a cheerful, uncomplaining boy who worked hard at all the strenuous training Meroot prepared for him, but he secretly learned to read. He was very musical—a gift Meroot thought wasted on a future soldier. It was lucky she did not know the hours he spent in our house playing any instrument he could lay his hands on. He composed tunes too and put words to them. There was one very special song he used to sing, a lullaby, the rhythm of which haunts me still.

"Where did you learn that?" I asked him. A slightly puzzled look came over his face.

"A woman taught it to me," he said. "A woman with fair hair like mine."

"Was she your nurse?"

Gamal hesitated. "I don't know," he said.

I knew by his air of embarrassment that there was something mysterious about the song that he himself could not explain.

Even apart from her treatment of Gamal, I never liked Meroot. She always *seemed* to be kind to me, drawing me to her and kissing me, stroking my hair, using flattering words, bringing me presents from her frequent travels, but there was something about her that made me uneasy. Her words sounded false, and I felt that though she claimed to love me, actually she didn't really like me at all. Once, when Gamal and I were about five, we were alone with her in her apartment having a quarrel over a toy, a wooden bird with moving wings. We shouted at each other and grabbed the bird back and forth between us. Suddenly Meroot leaned over, smacked me, snatched the toy from my grasp, and gave it to Gamal. The look she gave me was one of pure hatred, and I shrank back from her. I never trusted her after that.

Soon I realized that my mother's lips tightened whenever Meroot's name was mentioned and that she never entertained Meroot except on official occasions when her absence would have been noticed. Once when Aunt Meroot was away on one of her journeys and Gamal was happily living in our house, I said to my mother, "Wouldn't it be nice if Aunt Meroot never came back?" My mother laughed in a slightly rebuking way, as grownups do when they agree with you but don't want you to know it, and I could see that she felt just as I did, and that like me and Erith, she enjoyed spoiling Gamal as if to counteract Meroot's influence.

I spent a lot of time with my mother just then. Usually she was a woman who liked her own company, and she would sit contentedly for hours in her chamber reading or sewing. Yet when I wandered in from playing or riding my pony she seemed pleased to see me and we had long conversations together.

In one of these conversations I was surprised to discover that Meroot, just like Euny, was my godmother. I tried to get Erlain to discuss it, but she would say nothing except, "She is your father's sister." But her face was cold and her lips disapproving, and I guessed that the choice had not pleased her.

"Why is Meroot so nasty to Gamal?" I asked. "She makes him sleep in that cold room without proper blankets."

"She wants to make him a great warrior," Erlain replied.

"I can't be a great warrior," I said.

"No," she said, her eyes meeting mine, "you will need other powers."

"What other powers?"

"It is too soon to say."

"If I had a brother, would he rule the kingdom after Father?"

"Yes," said my mother, expressionless.

"But if I don't have a brother?"

"That would depend," she said. "On your power. The strength of the warrior is not the only kind."

I went out to the ditch to think things over, and

crouching against the grassy rampart, I wondered whether I had any power. I didn't feel as if I did, although I *had* used special powers to find water. I had not set out to use them, however. It had simply happened when I wasn't thinking about it. I couldn't see how that would be much use in running a kingdom, and I could well imagine that if my mother did not bear a son, a powerful knight or a distant cousin might take the kingdom over or . . . Gamal . . . !

Just as his name occurred to me, a pebble struck me lightly on the head, a shout came from above, and Gamal slithered down the bank beside me and landed with a bump at the bottom. It was as if thinking about him had brought him there.

"Gamal!"

"Mother's away and I've got the afternoon free from swordplay. Let's go somewhere."

The two of us saddled our ponies and rode away, galloping over the moorland toward the distant sea. We made for a little valley, quite deserted, where the horses moved down trails between the trees toward a stream that led to the sea. When we reached the sandy beach, we threw off our clothes and plunged into the waves. Afterward, sunning ourselves on the rocks, we played a game of seeing how long we could sit on one rock before the incoming tide engulfed us. We had the sense to know that if we waited too long it would be really dangerous, but it was fascinating to see how long the sea took, making occasional bold sallies farther up the beach and then, as if preparing to trick us, not moving in our direction for a long, long time.

"Will *you* become *regulus* of Cornwall when my father dies?" I asked Gamal bluntly. "Is that what Meroot wants?"

Gamal reddened. "It's what she wants. It doesn't mean it will happen." Then he added, "Your mother may have a son."

"And if she doesn't?"

Gamal shrugged. I considered for a bit, then remembered my mother's words.

"The strength of the warrior is not the only kind," I repeated. "There are other kinds of power. I intend to learn what they are and, as my father's daughter, rule after him."

Gamal gave me a long, thoughtful glance.

"I hope you do," he said. "As you know, I want to be a musician, not a ruler, though Mother would never let me." He stood up as if the game with the tide no longer interested him. "If you have the power to rule and do it rightly, you will have my allegiance and my fealty," he said. "I would be glad to serve you." He pretended to take an imaginary cap off his head and swept a low bow to me. Then he climbed on his horse and rode away.

I was surprised and touched by his response, by the love and faithfulness in his gray eyes, and by the fact that he had not mocked my claims to power. But I suddenly felt very weak and frightened.

IT WAS AROUND that period that I began to dream—a dream that always had the same ingredients, except that each time the action proceeded a little further, and each time I woke up with a worrying sense that there was something I should do about the dream, only I could not imagine what it was. This feeling was slight at first but grew stronger and stronger.

The first part of the dream was tranquil and beautiful. There was a hazel tree with a full moon hanging in the sky beyond it which lit its leaves and branches until they shone like jewels. This passed into a sense of flying in a night sky rich with stars. Up to this point the dream was delightful, but then suddenly I was in a dark tunnel. I was not alone—I was running, terror-stricken, with some other people, and there was a deafening sound in our ears that I could not identify—was it thunder? As if the noise were not bad enough, there was a most peculiar smell, as of a wild beast, which inspired a sense of fear. At my mother's suggestion I discussed this dream with one of our astrologers, but though my people thought dreams were very important, he seemed unwilling to ponder what it might mean. I think he was afraid that he might have to prophesy a terrible accident—or even worse—and he preferred not to think about it. So I struggled to think about it all by myself, but apart from remembering that hazel was the wood we had used to find water on the day the twig turned into a snake, I could make nothing of it.

As I grew older, I spent less time with Erith and more with my tutors and my mother. I liked learning most of the time, and I had the best of teachers. I had long outstripped Gamal, who spent most of his day in mock battles on the green enclosure where the men shot their arrows and wrestled and practiced with their weapons. Only in music, even though his fingers were tired and wrenched from his day's exercise, could he outshine me. He played beautifully upon the harp and flute, and he could sing well too, in a pure angelic treble. Most afternoons, sweaty, tired, hungry, he would come to see me after a day of wrestling or riding or swordplay. I too had finished my day's work—writing, translating, listening to my father giving judgment on a difficult case. Erith would bring both of us scented water in which to wash, and we would change our clothes. Then we ate some fruit or sweetmeats and settled down to play. Even Meroot did not forbid this. On wet days we played finchnell or made music. On fine days we walked or rode, coming home in the twilight to share a stew or roasted bird in front of the fire.

Together too we played with Moon, who liked to walk up our arms and sit on our shoulders. He had a way of apparently listening to our conversations, his head on one side, a thoughtful, judicial expression on his face that was irresistibly funny. Gamal often addressed questions to him, then replied in a pretend owl voice.

"*Isn't* Ninnoc in a bad temper today, Moon?" Gamal would ask, and then reply owlishly to himself, "I don't know what you're complaining about. I have to put up with her all the time."

Gamal and I had begun to share a secret. When, day by day, he returned from his labors as an apprentice soldier, he was often cut or bruised. He would have a long scratch down his face, a nasty graze on his leg, a pulled shoulder, a twisted ankle. To begin with I would bathe these injuries for him, put ointment on them, bandage them, until we began to notice something strange. The injuries began to grow better as soon as I looked at them or touched them, and often before I had reached for the bandage.

"Don't tell anyone!" I begged him, suddenly shy at this discovery.

"What is it that you do?" he asked me. That was the embarrassing part. I didn't *do* anything. I just looked at the sore place and touched it and did whatever was necessary to make it feel better.

"I wonder what you *couldn't* heal," Gamal went on. A week later we had the chance to find out. He came in with his arm broken after a bout of wrestling in which he had slipped and fallen. His tutor stood at the door waiting to take him to the bonesetter, but Gamal insisted on coming to me first. Seeing his face twisted with pain and the protective way he held his arm, I put out a hand and touched him with the utmost gentleness. This time, because it was so important to make him better, I concentrated really hard on healing his broken arm. Nothing happened. We had discovered the limit of my power. I could manage cuts, scratches, and bruises, but anything else was beyond me.

3

SINCE THE DAY when she had found me in the stable Euny had not spoken to me, which I thought was odd behavior for a godmother. Perhaps twice a year I would see her at Castle Dore, marching purposefully through the palace on her way to my father's apartments. I noticed that she would spend hours with him, but then scorn the feasting and the presents with which we regaled most of our visitors and leave as simply as she came, setting off on the long walk to the mysterious place where she lived in the Outland. I had no idea what she and my father could talk about.

One day, however, a change came. Erith entered the room where I was practicing my calligraphy—I remember that I was gilding a letter A that had a tiny blue man sitting sideways on the crossbar and swinging his leg—and said, "King Mark wants to see you. Right away." She turned sharply and went out. I sighed—I had been enjoying my work and was annoyed at being interrupted, but no one kept my father waiting. I suppose because that day changed my life I can still remember the look of the writing, the brilliant autumn sky, and even the gown I wore—blue, with a belt worked in precious stones and silk.

My father sat in the great chair that he used when he was meeting people officially. On a smaller chair beside him, very upright, sat Euny, who did not greet or notice me. I sat on an even smaller chair, suddenly feeling insignificant and shy.

"We have been talking," said my father, "Euny and I, about your future. As you know, it is the custom of this country to send a noble child away from home for a year or two to stay in another house as part of that child's education. It is usually boys who are sent, but in this case the circumstances are unusual. Euny, as your godmother, has proposed that in, say, a year's time, we should send you to live with her for a while. She believes, and I agree with her, that she will have valuable lessons to teach you."

The expression on my face must have betrayed my horror at the idea of living with Euny, because my father frowned sternly at me. I had forgotten that however startled I was, he expected me to show good manners.

"Go away from here!" I said. "From Erith and you and Mother and Gamal and everyone? To go and live *in the Outland?*"

"You will come to no harm."

I was so upset that I felt my lower lip begin to droop

with the threat of tears. Euny spoke, but she was not in the least reassuring.

"It is necessary," she said. "There are things you need to learn—things only I can teach you. I am your godmother, and I claim the right to instruct you."

"I don't want to go," I said sullenly, half under my breath.

"For a year and a day," Euny went on as if I had not spoken. "That should do it. You will come to me in about a year. I shall not send for you—you will know when the moment comes. Come alone, on foot, with a few clothes. That should suffice."

"Very well, then," said my father. "It's settled." I knew that this was the signal for me to leave, and unwillingly I got up to go. Euny followed me, and when we were outside the door, she turned to me with a rather wolfish smile, hissing through her teeth the one word, "Juniper!" almost as if she were making a joke. Then she turned and walked away.

I was deeply shaken by this encounter. I discussed it with Erith, who was indignant at the suggestion that I should go anywhere without her, and I mentioned it to my mother, Erlain, who was sympathetic but who, predictably, sided with my father. However, she shed a new light on the idea.

"We have spoken of the power you may need one day," she said. "I think it is too soon to say whether you will have that, or should use it, but Euny is one who has power. That is why we chose her for you as a godmother. She is quite right—you could learn from her."

This made the whole idea seem a little better, but at

the same time I dreaded leaving all the places and people I knew and going to live in the Outland.

"What is Euny's house like?" I asked sulkily.

"I don't know. I have never been there. I've heard that it is beside a great hill—a tor—near the sea, and I think she appoints herself a sort of guardian of the hill."

This was comforting in a way—I liked the idea of living by the sea—but I was still puzzled. And hurt.

"You will send me to the Outland to stay at a house you have never seen? The Outland is *dangerous*—everybody knows that. I might easily be killed by brigands or by our enemies. None of you seems to care. And Euny is so dirty and horrible."

Quite apart from the dangers of the Outland, I could not understand why my parents trusted Euny so much. I did not like Euny, nor trust her, and I was afraid of her rags and poverty.

My mother hesitated.

"The Christians say that there is no magic—that the world is ruled by love. I cannot decide whether they are right. Our forebear Arthur was a Christian yet believed in magic," she said. "*This* kingdom seems to be controlled by magic, good magic and bad magic. For those who choose the good magic it is important to have strong allies who choose good magic too. Euny is your father's strongest ally. If you let her, she will become your ally, and that may be important."

Erlain said all this very gravely, and though the words she used were simple, it was as if she were talking to a grownup. Somehow, without really understanding, I knew that I would have to go to be Euny's pupil.

I wondered when. Euny had said in about a year and

that I would know when the time came, but I could not imagine how. In any case, a year seemed a comfortably long time away.

AUTUMN SLIPPED into a snowy winter, and little seemed to have changed in my life. Except one thing. The dream of the hazel tree was coming more and more often. Always I was delighted by its beauty—it filled me with a sort of hunger that was also a kind of joy, the feeling that if I could find it I would be supremely happy. Occasionally I woke up at this point and there were tears of happiness on my cheeks. But far more often I was back again in the tunnel, running in terror from the dreadful fate that pursued me and my companions and which was heralded by the intolerable noise and smell.

I told Gamal about the conversation with Euny. He was so fascinated that he went right home and told Meroot. Later he said that she was "very angry" about it. I could not understand why it would make Meroot angry, but I was not in the least sorry that it did.

I grew a lot in that year and felt as if I came to understand many more things. I played the harp every day, I learned and sang many of the famous songs of my people, I studied the stars and learned astrological law, I read Latin and wrote what I believed was a beautiful script. More often my father took me into his council chamber when he was listening to a dispute and afterward would ask me what I thought of his decision. I usually got bored in the middle of all the explanations, though, and went off into a daydream. I daydreamed a lot at that time. Sometimes I daydreamed that I was a beautiful woman whom everybody adored, sometimes that I was a brave soldier who was afraid of nothing.

One day something odd happened, as odd as the day when I had felt the twig move in my hands. It was a bright spring morning and Gamal and I had run away, in my case from lessons and in Gamal's from the perpetual wearisome drilling of his life as a boy-soldier. We were riding a long way from Castle Dore in the Outland territory, which my father had forbidden to us. We were cantering in a wide grassy space with trees on one side of it. I knew from previous experience that a bit farther the ground rose steeply, passed into a narrow gully by a stream with cliffs on both sides, swung toward a narrow place where you could pass only one at a time, and then opened toward an estuary and the sea.

I suppose I was thinking about the place, anticipating it, when suddenly, with total clarity, I saw it in my mind's eye. On the far side of the narrow gorge was a camp with ragged women and children and skinny horses grazing. But in the narrow place between the rocks several men were crouched holding weapons, clearly with the intention of killing or holding for ransom anyone who attempted to pass. So vivid was this picture that I had to look around me to make sure that I was not actually at the gorge. No, there was the spacious stretch of grass, the trees, and the lithe movement of our horses beneath us. But there we were, it seemed to me, heading fast toward danger.

At once I told myself I was making up a story and

that I must order my thoughts, but then, as if from beside me, came a voice, very like the owlish voice in which Gamal imitated Moon. "Don't go . . . don't go." On that day, as on many others, I was carrying Moon asleep in my pocket. I slowed my horse, and though I knew the owl hated bright daylight I pulled him out. He fluffed his feathers, blinked crossly, and said again (I could see his beak moving), "Don't go . . . don't go."

"You can talk, Moon!" I said.

"Of course," he replied wearily. "But now I want to go back to sleep."

I shouted to Gamal to stop, reined in my horse, and slipped to the ground. Gamal rode back to me, puzzled. He was even more puzzled when I told him.

"You just made that up!" he said.

"Perhaps I did. I'm not sure. But I am quite certain that if we ride through the gorge we will be in danger."

Gamal chewed thoughtfully on a piece of grass.

"In that case, how about climbing that path up above the gorge—you remember the one—and looking down on the camp? Just to see."

I did not want to appear cowardly, so I swallowed my longing to turn and go home and set off with him on foot along a path through the trees. There was something very reassuring about having an adventure with Gamal. He had such a sensible, cheerful air as he stalked along in front of me, once or twice stopping to listen carefully. As we approached the head of the gorge, we became very quiet indeed—I knew that Gamal must really have believed what I had told him. Then we were in sight of the place where the gorge, that huge split in the surface of the earth, began. We stole lightly across to the rock that overlooked the gorge and stared down. All was just as I had seen it! I was about to gloat over this when I glanced to one side. A hundred paces away two robber scouts were staring intently at us and beginning to move in our direction!

"Gamal!" I hissed. "Run. Run!" Both of us turned back to the woods and ran, fleet of foot, driven by the sound of the robbers crashing through the undergrowth behind us. Our only hope was the two horses tethered where we had left them. In spite of our start the robbers were not very far behind when we leaped into our saddles and urged our horses away. Catching our panic, they took off at full speed, manes and tails flowing in the wind. I looked around once and saw one of the robbers about to fit an arrow into his bow. I did not look again.

After that, Gamal was inclined to be respectful of my gifts but to wonder why I had foreseen the robbers in the gorge but did not know about the robber scouts. I could not tell him.

"Can all women do magic?" he asked me.

"I don't think so," I replied.

"Meroot can, you know," he said.

"What kind?"

"I'm not sure. She won't talk about it. It's just that I see her books and parchments. There's a terrifying picture in one of them . . . And sometimes she mixes potions." He sounded unhappy.

"What sort of picture?" I was intrigued.

"There was someone drinking something and falling asleep . . ." Gamal spoke unwillingly. "Then they were in a coffin buried in the ground, but alive, awake, fighting to get out. It gave me nightmares for weeks."

"You think people . . . you think *Meroot* would do a thing like that to her enemies?" I asked, frightened.

"I don't know," Gamal said wretchedly.

"I don't really understand magic," I said. "That's why I'm going to Euny's, I suppose."

"Do you want to go?"

"I don't know."

Somehow that day made me feel that I needed to be taught whatever it was Euny knew. Perhaps, I thought, she could teach me really effective magic and I would be able to use it to make people do anything I wanted them to do. That was a pleasing thought. In any case, I felt myself moving inevitably toward her—even though I didn't like her much. It was very odd.

"So how is it," Gamal persisted, "that if you can see into the future you cannot beat me at finchnell? You should be able to see my moves several turns ahead."

"I do beat you sometimes," I said indignantly, but I saw his point. There was something that didn't make sense.

Now that I had discovered that Moon could speak I spent a lot of time talking to him, but to my disappointment he did not utter another sound. He would gaze at me very intelligently with his head to one side or sit blinking his amber eyes, but that was all.

"Please say something, Moon," I would beg. "I know

you can." But he simply ruffled his feathers and blinked at me with those astonishing eyes.

One night I dreamed again of the hazel tree and the tunnel. This time whatever was pursuing me was close at hand. I woke up after the dream, and the feeling of fear was very great, though it was gradually succeeded by a longing for the hazel tree. I knew that something had to change, but I could not imagine what it might be.

4

THE NEXT MORNING I woke at dawn, shivering and sweating from my dreams, and for the first time I knew what I must do. I got straight out of bed and began to prepare a bundle for myself. I put in two of my simplest smocks and chose another to wear, with a large pocket that could accommodate my owl. I included a bone comb that had been a present from my mother, sandals, and a cloak. I wrapped a shawl around my shoulders and put on the boots I wore in wet weather. I was very tempted to leave without saying good-bye to my parents or Erith, but I feared that if I did, there would be a hue and cry in search of me. So I sat down to wait until the rest of the household was awake.

My parents were breakfasting when I entered their apartments. Erlain looked distressed when I told her that the day of my departure had come, yet all the same I believe she thought that I was right to go.

"We shall miss you," she said, "but I shall think of you every day. Be my brave girl and learn whatever Euny can teach you. And remember, it is only for a year and a day. Not *such* a long time." It seemed a very long time to me. My father kissed me warmly but said little. I felt that he did not like the parting, yet trusted Euny and her conviction that I needed to learn from her.

The person who made the greatest fuss was Erith, who wept and hugged me and wrung her hands in a truly heartbreaking way.

"I'm coming *back*, Erith," I kept explaining, but she did not seem to think that helped at all. In the end I gave up trying to comfort her—it only made *me* want to cry. I picked up my bundle and simply walked out the door. Once safely away from the Wooden Palace, I felt much more cheerful; it was very pleasant walking along in the morning's coolness. There was an autumn bite in the air that made me move quickly, but I felt full of energy, as if I could walk forever. After about an hour I heard the sound of hoofs behind me on the path, and looking back, I saw Gamal following me. When he got closer I could see that he was angry but trying to hide it.

"You went away without saying good-bye to me."

"I am sorry, but I only decided to go this morning, and by then I knew you would be out on the field practicing. I asked Erlain to say good-bye for me."

"She did, so I just left the field. Old Talan's in a rage."

I thought Gamal was rather brave. Meroot had punished him severely the last time he had run away from his tutors to ride with me.

"I'll have to go back, but I was determined to say good-bye." He slid off his horse and gave me an awkward, boyish kiss. "I hope you'll be happy with Euny. She looks like a bit of an ogress to me."

"I'll miss you."

Unable to think of anything else to say, Gamal mounted his horse and soon disappeared toward home. I missed him the moment he was out of sight; now, instead of feeling light and exhilarated, as I had when I set out, I felt sad and lonely. I continued my journey more slowly.

As the day wore on, it became hot—a dazzling September day. After I had walked for several hours my feet became sore, and I took off my boots and walked in the dust, which felt silky and comforting. Foolishly, I had not thought to bring any water with me, so I drank out of the wayside streams. Later, however, I became very hungry and wondered why I had forgotten to bring bread. I found a few berries.

I was not very sure of the way, but I had a sort of landmark. Once on a trip I had made with my father, he had pointed out to me an odd-shaped hill in the distance. "That's where Euny lives," he had said. I could see the hill, purple-black, away in the distance, a hill that rose sheer out of a flat landscape. Sometimes I lost sight of it as I passed through woods or along deep leafy tracks, but then it would reappear and I would know that I was not lost. For a long time, though, it did not seem to get any closer.

In the late afternoon I came to a great forest that lay between me and the hill. I knew that forests were dangerous for unarmed travelers—that there might be boars or wolves or outlaws who lived there, and I feared being eaten or robbed and killed. I sat down in despair on the edge of the forest and wondered what to do. It would be a sad end to my journey to die in the forest—I was much too young to die, I thought.

Despite my fears I found it very beautiful in the forest, with the tawny autumn colors glowing like fires, and away in the distance the dim blue light of the dying day. I had discovered one of the broad roads that ran through the forest, and it seemed to me that if I stuck to the road (and it was going in the right direction), I might be safe, though once when I heard someone approaching I hid in the bushes. It was a party of monks, and I thought of coming out and asking for their protection, but then it occurred to me that they might disapprove of Euny, so I stayed in my hiding place. It was growing cold in the forest and I shivered in my shawl. I knew that it would be dark before long, and I fervently wanted to be out of the forest before nightfall.

Just as if I were being taken care of, I stepped out of the forest as the first stars were coming out. I was on a path that led straight toward the mysterious hill. I walked on, very tired now, the hill slowly looming larger between me and the sky yet still a long way off. I thought I could hear the distant grumble of the sea. I was cold and stiff from the walk, my legs were scratched and bleeding, and my bundle felt heavy, yet I kept going, one foot after the other. I sang to myself to keep up my spirits and looked at the great stars above me. Suddenly, as if time had compressed itself, I stood at the foot of the great hill. Now, I thought, if I walked around it, I would find Euny's house.

This was not as easy as it sounds. There were deep ditches and streams, little coppices, and high walls of bushes. Although I could dimly see the stepping stones over the stream, I was so tired that I stumbled right into it and fell full-length into the water. I gasped at the bitter cold and then staggered out, my clothes dripping and my flesh shivering in the night wind. I was past crying; I was simply trying to endure in order to reach Euny. When I drew poor little Moon out of my pocket he was ruffling his wet feathers indignantly. I thought it might make him cross enough to say something, but he did not speak. Nor did he speak when a bit later I fell heavily down a bank, hurting my ankle and scraping my arm.

"Euny! Euny!" I had begun to say out loud. It was just then that a crescent moon swung into view over a clearing, and in its gentle light, black against the sky and the curve of the hill, I saw a little hut with firelight showing under the door. I did not know whether it was the house I sought, but I knew that I could go no farther. I stumbled toward it and pressed the latch. The door swung open on a small square room. Between me and the fire was a rocking chair with someone sitting in it who did not turn around.

"So Juniper decided to come after all, did she?" said Euny's voice. "Shut the door behind you—there's a terrible draft."

TWO

5

SHIVERING and exhausted, I crept toward the fire as an animal would have done and sank down before it. I must have looked a terrible sight—my hair and clothes sopping wet, my limbs covered in blood and mud, my ankle beginning to swell. If Euny had uttered one word of sympathy I would have burst into a flood of tears. Instead she sat in silence, perfectly still. After a bit she said, "There's a blanket on the bed," and eventually it occurred to me that she meant me to strip off my damp clothes and wrap myself in it. I looked around the room. There was a box bed in one corner, and I went over and took out the ragged blanket and put it around my cold shoulders. Meanwhile Euny had filled a bowl with soup from the fire and set it in the hearth for me.

I put a hand out of my blanket, grasped the battered spoon she gave me, and ate the soup. It had odd bits of gristle in it and the strange flavor that I was to discover Euny's soup often had, but it sent a shiver of delight through me. It was hot and spicy, and I could feel some faint flicker of energy return to my exhausted body.

"There won't be much food to eat here," Euny said, "so you needn't expect it."

What I was wondering at that moment was where I was going to sleep. I had always slept in a bed with down pillows and linen sheets. I could see that there would be no room for me in Euny's tiny bed.

"Please, where shall I sleep?" I asked at last.

"On the hearth, of course," said Euny. "This isn't a palace, you know." She managed to inject a lot of scorn into that remark. She got up, went across the room, and fetched a furry skin. It had an odd smell that I didn't like at all.

"This will keep you warm," she said.

Now I had another problem. Every night of my life Erith had helped me take off my clothes, brushed my hair, and tucked me into bed. Every morning she had bathed me, dressed me, and braided my hair for me. I had no idea how to do any of it for myself. It had not occurred to me that anyone dressed and undressed without help.

"Please, will you help me undress?" I asked.

Euny laughed, a bark of a laugh, not altogether unkind, and without a word went back to her rocking chair. I realized with astonishment that she had no intention of giving me any help. With humiliating difficulty I managed to get my clothes off and comb my hair. I remembered that the little owl was still in my pocket, so I took him out, stood him on a beam, and fed him a tidbit of mouse I had brought from home. I was nervous that this would provoke further rudeness from Euny, but to my surprise a broad smile spread across her face.

"How just like you!" she said as if she were laughing at a private joke. Since she scarcely knew me, I could not see how she knew whether it was like me or not.

Later I lay curled up in Euny's fur rug, half of it beneath me, protecting me from the cold of the flagstones, half of it above me. Now that I was inside it the smell was overpowering. My head lolled uncomfortably on one of the creature's paws. There was warmth from the fire, though the shifting of the ashes disturbed me at first. Tired as I was, I went quickly to sleep but woke long before dawn, cold and miserable and hating the sound of Euny's snores from across the room. It seemed to me that I might have made a terrible mistake—that although Euny had told me to come, she was not glad, as I had expected her to be. In any case, I would never survive the discomfort and squalor of life there, with no one to dress me and take care of me. Great tears of self-pity ran down my cheeks.

I sat up, my body cramped and frozen. It was not light yet, but I could leave as soon as it was dawn. My torn smock, hanging over the rocking chair near the fire, had dried in the night. I had simply to dress and leave before Euny woke. Just then, however, my ankle jarred with pain as I moved. I could see that badly swollen as it was, I would never manage the long walk home. I groaned and curled back again into the strong-smelling skin.

I must have dozed, because the next thing I knew, it was light, and I could hear Euny moving around and smell ham frying.

"Thought you'd be hungry this morning," said Euny. "This is the last of the old pig—it's a bit high, but it'll do you good. We'll kill the next pig before winter." She handed me a plate—it didn't look like a very clean plate to me—with a bit of fried ham and a hunk of black bread on it. She was quite right, I *was* very hungry, and although the ham had a rancid taste I gulped it down together with the black bread and some lumpy porridge she was stirring over the fire.

"I can see you'll eat me out of house and home," Euny said in her cross voice. "Get dressed, wash yourself, comb your hair, try to look like a human being even if you can't look like a princess."

Obediently, though very slowly and awkwardly, I washed myself clean in the freezing water, combed my tangly hair, put on another of the smocks in my bundle, and tied on my sandals. I was surprised to find that I could do it all by myself.

"Now sit down," said Euny. "We need to talk."

Stiff and tired from my long walk and my night among the ashes, and still rather hungry, I sat miserably down, my swollen ankle in front of me.

Before we talked, Euny selected some herbs and tied them around my ankle.

"Walk on it," she said, "but not too much." My ankle hurt badly with each step I took.

"Now," she said, "I expect you feel very hard done by this morning, living in this miserable hole after the splendors of the palace." She sounded as if she were gloating, and I was too angry to trust myself to speak. Children in my country are trained to be very polite to grownups.

"But I am a poor person—not rich like your father—and this is the way poor people live."

I knew, because Erlain had told me, that Euny had been offered a house at the Wooden Palace and all kinds of presents by my father, but that she had always refused.

As if she guessed my thoughts, Euny went on. "I find life easier this way. Let me tell you why I think you are here. I won't talk much about it after today, so listen carefully. What I know about is power. Not the sort of power your father has with soldiers and armies and weapons, but a power that comes from knowing—"

"I know a lot," I said, eager to please. "I know Latin, and about the stars, and mathematics, and poems . . ."

"Not that sort of knowing," she said, interrupting me rather contemptuously. "That sort just gets in the way—makes you think you are clever, like weapons make men think they are strong. My sort of power is about *seeing*—seeing into the future, seeing into someone's heart and mind. Sometimes it is about knowing what a tribe or people must do to escape danger. Sometimes it is just about understanding yourself or

one other person. Seeing and knowing—and being very
truthful about what you see and know—they make things
begin to happen, maybe more things than battles and
armies. Sometimes they prevent bad things." I thought
of the moment with Gamal on the hillside but did not
feel like mentioning it.

"So could I have power?" I asked.

"It is too soon to say. It is possible. But you may
spoil it."

"How?" I asked anxiously.

"By wanting it too much. Or by using it badly."

"And if I don't spoil it?"

"Then you will become what the powerful ones call
a *doran*. And that might be very important for your
father and his kingdom. But it is a long, difficult path
and it may be too much for you."

"It won't," I said, determined not to miss my chance.

"Or you may decide you don't like the idea when
you know more about it."

I thought that was very unlikely. I remembered
Gamal's question.

"Is it only women who become *doran*s?" I asked her.

"No. But there are more women who take that path.
Men prefer to put their trust in weapons and fighting.
They don't know it, but it makes them weaker."

Asking Gamal's question had reminded me of something else.

"Is Meroot a *doran?*" I asked Euny. Her face dark-
ened and her lip curled with scorn.

"Meroot only uses magic to make other people do
what she wants."

I remembered my own fantasies of doing just that.

"Is that bad?" I asked timidly.

"It is *wicked*," Euny replied with a terrifying emphasis. Then, with the air of one who has had more conversation than she is used to, Euny stood up and packed some bread into a basket before hoisting it onto her back.

"I have work to do today," she said, "so you'll just have to stay here. Light the fire and make some soup for supper. I'm not sure if I'll be back by nightfall."

6

WHEN EUNY had gone I spent a little while sitting glumly in her rocking chair, my sore ankle propped up in front of me. Now that I was alone I examined the room in more detail. There were the ashes of the fire and hanging above it the chain, which held a griddle and a kettle. There also hung a large piece of mutton, left to blacken in the peat smoke. That, and no doubt the tallow lamp made from mutton fat, gave the hut an unpleasant smell. Beside the fire was a basket of peats, a little brush for cleaning the hearth, the lamp on a shelf, and a small stool. In addition to the rocking chair, the skin rug, and the bed, the room contained a rickety table and an upright chair, a rather dirty woven rug, a bowl and jug, some cups and plates on a simple dresser, a hand mill with meal spilling out of the top, and a jug with some milk. In a corner stood a woodpile with some sticks lying on top and a tinderbox on the floor beside it.

There were dried plants hanging from the ceiling and the remains of the pig's carcass. Euny owned nothing, it occurred to me, that was not absolutely necessary to keep her warm or fed, and I thought with wonder of the way she had refused my father's offer of money and possessions. The books, the musical instruments, the goblets, the jewels, and the fine clothes to which I had been accustomed at home seemed unimaginable here.

What was I to do with myself all day? Euny had gone and might not be back till the morrow and there was I, all alone with nothing at all to do and only able to walk with difficulty.

As so often since the day out with Gamal, I tried to talk to Moon, but he did not stir from his daytime sleep. I had never before lit a fire or attempted to cook, but because I was cold and would soon be hungry again, I thought I had better learn how. I thought it might be easier to light a fire of wood than of peat. I placed some big pieces of wood in the hearth and set some moss on top of them. Then I struck at the flint. Even when the sparks fell on the dry moss, the little fire-seeds gradually faded. I tried time after time, feeling more and more irritated. After a bit it occurred to me that the twigs might light more easily than the wood. This time I transferred the moss to the twigs; the twigs sizzled a little, and I thought that maybe the fire would light, but still I did not succeed.

I sat back on the rocking chair and looked despairingly at the cold hearth. Other people could light fires. Why was I so stupid? Then I remembered seeing ser-

vants at home sweeping up the ashes and carrying them
away. Without much hope of it making a difference, I
took down my pyramid of wood, cleared away the ashes
with a shovel that lay beside the hearth, relaid the fire,
and repeated the procedure with the tinderbox. This
time, to my delight, the twigs flared up, making a generous blaze, and soon the logs were aflame. I felt very
proud of myself.

There was still some soup left in the cauldron, and
although it was only midmorning, I heated it up and
ate it with some black bread that I had found on the
dresser. I noticed the same odd taste that I had noted
the night before. I later discovered that Euny had a
way of throwing whatever food she had into her soup,
not just bread and cheese but meat or even offal together with any herbs that came to hand. It did not
always taste nice. But I would have to devise another
soup for our evening meal.

My hunger appeased, I went out to look at the pig
and the chickens Euny kept. The pig was a huge black
beast that lived in a sty behind the hut; its grunts and
snufflings had disturbed me more than once during the
night. The chickens' white feathers looked dirty and
bedraggled, but I was glad to notice that several eggs
were already lying inside the henhouse, and I carefully
collected them. I saw that Euny was growing some beans
and flax and some bere corn. There were two stunted
apple trees with a few apples left on the boughs.

Time hung very heavily on my hands for the rest of
that day. I talked a bit to Moon, hoping as always that
he would reply or even give me some advice, but he

merely blinked and went back to sleep. Limping painfully, I drew some water from Euny's well, washed out
the smock I had worn the day before, and hung it over
the chair to dry. I washed my hair too and let it dry in
the bright, warm noontime sunshine. I carefully ar-
ranged blocks of peat on the fire and loved the smell
as the fire reached them. Mindful of the charge to make
some soup, I managed to persuade a little more meat
from the pig's carcass and added some water and herbs
and a little meal, but it was a poor, thin broth. When
darkness fell I ate the soup with a couple of the eggs
and the rest of the black bread and some milk, reluc-
tantly saving what was left of the milk for the next
morning. Before going to bed I built up the fire as
much as possible, and wrapping myself once more in
the strange-smelling animal skin, I lay down before the
hearth.

The fire threw alarming shadows onto the walls of
the hut. The silence outside felt ominous to me. Except for the occasional scream of a rabbit caught by a
stoat or a fox, I could hear nothing at all, but I imag-
ined outlaws surrounding the hut, preparing to break
into it. Because of my fears and the discomfort of the
floor, I slept very badly—the shifting and sighing of
the fire disturbed me. There was a growing feeling of
cold as the night drew on. "I don't like this at all," I
thought, "no matter how much power I get out of it,
nor how important it is to be a *doran*. I'd rather marry
the son of a neighboring prince, or even the son of one
of the knights, as all the other girls do. That would be
much better than spending my life cold and hungry in

a place like this. As soon as Euny returns I will tell her, and then when my ankle is better I will go back home." Feeling that I had settled something, I rearranged the skin and sank into a sound sleep. I was woken several hours later by Euny lifting the latch and entering the hut.

7

ALTHOUGH I HAD decided so firmly to leave
Euny, I found it difficult to get around to telling her about it, perhaps because I was a little
afraid of her. Maybe too, I thought that some marvelous thing might still happen that would make it worth-
while to live there.

On the second morning, when I woke up cold and
stiff, Euny decided promptly that my ankle was better,
though it felt far from better to me, and sent me out
before breakfast to collect two buckets of water from
her well, to gather sticks and relight the fire, and to
wash my face in the cold water and comb my hair. All
this before our very meager breakfast of porridge.

"Please, what I am going to give Moon?" I asked her
anxiously. At the Wooden Palace, I had always begged
the contents of the mousetraps from the cook, or she
had given me other scraps left over from our meals.

"There are plenty of field mice around here. Let him

go and hunt for himself," said Euny. I looked up anxiously at Moon. Suppose he starved because it did not
occur to him to seek his own food?

Actually I was still fairly hungry myself, though trying
hard not to notice it. I thought that we would now
settle down to lessons as I would have done at home,
only in something much more interesting, like spells,
but it didn't turn out that way. After a brisk tidying up
of the hut (that is, I tidied it while Euny looked on and
made sarcastic comments), we went out for an interminable walk in which Euny sought roots for some
medicine she wanted to make. It was a chill, windy day
and we marched for hours over meadows and through
woods. Every now and then, for no reason that I could
see, Euny would point to a plant that looked like all
the others and order me to dig it up. Some of them
had deep, tough roots, which she insisted I must dig
up intact. I had no tool apart from a stick and my fingers, and in no time my pretty nails were full of earth,
and my hands and smock were filthy. The only time
she spoke was to give me long explanations of what the
roots were and what they might be used for, which I
promptly forgot.

In contrast to Euny, who walked lightly and quickly,
looking about her as if everything were interesting and
must be noticed, I shuffled along, sullen and miserable,
until I began to take refuge in comforting daydreams.

"How many birds?" Euny asked suddenly.

"How do you mean?"

"There was a row of birds sitting on a branch. How
many?"

Of course I had no idea. I had not even seen the birds.

This unpleasant trick, I was soon to discover, was a favorite one of Euny's. She was given to precise, detailed questions. What color was the roof? What color *exactly* had the sky been? What direction was the wind blowing from? What animals had I noticed? Where were they? What flowers had I seen? She would ask, but I never knew the answers. It made me feel very silly.

What I was thinking about was not the number of birds nor the direction of the wind but the bliss of returning to the comforts of Castle Dore. I reflected that as the winter came on, life, which was already hard at Euny's, would become intolerable, with the cold, hard floor feeling even colder at night and the hunger becoming even more painful. It would be lonely too. I had been with Euny only a day and a half, and already I was missing Erith and my parents and other children to talk to. It was at this point I remembered that, after all, it was Euny who had asked me to come, and I thought that perhaps, as I was her godchild, she held some affection for me that she found difficult to show.

"Did you . . . sort of . . . want me to come?" I asked her timidly in the middle of a dark forest. I hoped for some sort of declaration from her that she loved me and was pleased that I was coming to live with her.

"It's all one to me," she said disappointingly.

But there was something even more fundamental that I needed to know, only I scarcely knew how to ask the question.

"I know what you said yesterday, but I still don't see

how I . . . what you . . . what I am here for," I got out at last. Euny gave a heavy sigh as if this were an unreasonable bit of curiosity on my part.

"Earth, air, fire, water," she said, and stopped.

"Like my rhyme," I said with interest, remembering my neck charm.

"Well, there you are."

I didn't seem to be anywhere.

"There are . . . things I can do," I said. "I can find water hidden underground, I can heal people—sometimes. I can see into the future, and once I thought I heard Moon speak."

"Don't boast!" she said sharply.

"But what does it *mean?*"

"It means that you must do exactly what I tell you!"

To make it all worse it began to rain during the afternoon, but in spite of that we did not make for home. Cold and wet, with the rain plastering my hair to my head, carrying the full basket of roots, hungry because we had not eaten since that meager plate of porridge at breakfast, I stumbled along behind Euny, now with my mind fully made up. Tomorrow I would get up early, while Euny was still asleep, grab my things, and set off for home. I might even leave my things behind, I reflected, in case collecting them would wake Euny. After all, there were plenty more clothes at home. I pictured Erith's rapturous welcome and all the sympathy I would get as I told my story, though I also felt a spasm of shame that I did not quite understand.

I was very tired now, and the long day's walk had caused my ankle to swell again. It was dark by the time we got to our own forest, but Euny entered it without hesitation and kept up a steady pace that, exhausted as I was, I found hard to match. I could think of nothing but sleep—my former raging appetite had died down now. When we came out of the forest there was a moon that showed the stepping stones across the stream as bright as day. It swam huge and golden over the shoulder of the tor and outlined the roof of Euny's hut. This was magical enough—a scene so beautiful that in spite of my exhaustion I felt transfixed by it—but there was something more. Standing between the tor and the hut, its branches silvered by the moonlight, quivering a little in the night breeze, stood the hazel tree I remembered from my dreams. My tiredness and hunger forgotten, I stood still and stared at the tree, stammering with excitement.

"The hazel tree. The tree in the dream. It's *here*."

To which Euny, to whom I had said nothing about my dream, replied, "Well, of course. It's been here all along. You could have noticed it by daylight if you weren't so absent-minded. You'll have to do better than that." And she went on into the hut.

As I stood, still transfixed by my discovery, I heard the brush of wings overhead and looked up to see Moon, white and ghostlike, flying above me, seeking his food just as Euny had recommended.

"Moon!" I called to him softly. "I have found the hazel tree!" At which he circled around me twice in acknowledgment before continuing on his hunting trail.

8

AND SO MY LIFE with Euny began. She was an odd mixture of busyness and laziness. She did not care at all about the state of the hut and spent most of the day sitting in her chair in front of the fire, sometimes asleep, sometimes humming tunelessly, sometimes just still and quiet. Yet she had periods of extraordinary energy. Alone or taking me with her, she would walk for long distances, as on that first dreadful day (walking so quickly that I found I was out of breath trying to keep up). Often she was making for a hill, a forest, a ring of trees or of stones. Once there she would search diligently for some particular spot— I could never work out where it was going to be—and having found it would stay, singing a wild tuneless song, muttering words that sounded like poems. Her eyes would be closed, her face set and concentrated. She smiled to herself quite often, but sometimes her expression would change to one of pain. She never said anything to me before or after these occasions, just let me stand there on whatever windswept hill or moorland we happened to be, shivering and rather frightened. I wanted to ask her to explain these times to me but I never had the courage.

Soon after my arrival we had climbed our own tor— its sides were steep and gaunt like the ribs of a giant, and I arrived at the top with my heart pounding. I could see our tiny hut a mere speck at the bottom, and there was a wonderful view of forest and hill, with the tor of Glasweryn and a village with its plowed fields away in the distance. On this occasion Euny neither laughed nor wept but simply stood quietly. Then she led me to a small wattle-and-daub hut that stood on the crest of the hill. Within it, like a queen in a hovel, was an extraordinary carved and painted figure set in a kind of cave made of stone. Her face was black, her eyes dark and wild, and upon her head she wore a crown decorated with a moon and stars. Her gown was blue and red, and sitting upon her lap was a baby, awkward and doll-like. A wreath of hedgerow flowers—the last beautiful flowers of autumn entwined with berries— had been hung around her neck, and others were strewn at her feet or thrust into little pots. At her feet was a well, its ancient wooden lid beautifully carved with flowers and animals. There were candles too, set around the rim of the well, one or two still alight, the others burned out as if many people had visited the place and left a burning candle as a memento of their visit.

Euny, always so dry, so caustic, astounded me by suddenly prostrating herself on the floor while I stood awkwardly by. When she got up I saw that her face was wet with tears. Then she opened the well, threw in the dipper on its long chain, drank a little of the water, and replaced the dipper without offering any water to me. On the way back to the hut she was silent. Only when we had nearly reached it did she say sternly to me, "You are not to climb the tor, nor visit the place of the Mother unless I tell you to." Immediately I felt irritated and as if I might wish to do so, though that steep climb would not otherwise have been much of a temptation.

In fact, Euny was full of instructions about what I might and might not do. From the moment she woke me each day from my uncomfortable sleep, usually very early in the morning, she ordered me out to draw water, to grind meal, to start up the fire, to make porridge, to gather sticks, to sweep, to feed the chickens, and to chop up scraps for the pig. I did not much mind doing these things since they helped us to keep warm or fed, or meant that the plates and pots were cleaner than when *she* washed them; it did annoy me, however, to see her sitting in her rocking chair, not helping, while I swept or cooked or cleaned the ashes from the fire or staggered in with the pails of water. It made me feel that I was her servant, which I didn't like at all. Once, on a bad day, I mumbled my resentment at her, and she replied with one of her crows of glee, "Yes, you are my servant. That is exactly what you are." My only comfort was that I did at least keep the hut cleaner than she did and that I soon learned to cook nicer meals.

THE TWO MOST painful things about life with Euny, however, were cold and hunger. In my privileged life in the Wooden Palace there had always been a fire blazing on the hearth, and I had always been warmly dressed and well fed. Life in the hut was very different. The thin walls did not keep in the warmth of our fire, and every night I woke up shivering, so that I felt tired and miserable the next day. As the winter approached, I went out gloveless in all weather on my innumerable errands for Euny, and my cloak and boots, made for life at Castle Dore, were not thick enough to keep out the damp and the cold. Soon I had chilblains on my hands and feet, which became very sore and drove me half mad with irritation whenever I did get warm. Euny showed no sympathy for my shivers or my chilblains. Once when I complained she said, "You came here to make your life real. Cold, hunger, the hard floor to lie on—these are your teachers."

If they were my teachers, I reflected angrily, then they made me very miserable. Yet I could not help noticing when I next picked up my spoon to eat my soup that since I had had almost no food all day, the soup tasted better than any soup I had ever eaten in my life. It was as if my whole body had suddenly come alive and was singing. The flavor of every bean, grain, and vegetable in the soup spoke to me. Even the water I drank tasted wonderful. Was it just the purity of Euny's well, or was it that desperately hungry as I was, my mouth was wonderfully alert to enjoy all that entered it?

Similarly, when I came in half frozen from a series of trips to the well, there was a special kind of joy in letting the warmth of the fire steal through my cold body, though the torment of the chilblains spoiled it a little.

It also occurred to me that I had never noticed the change from autumn to winter as sharply as I did now. Before, I was dimly aware, as everyone is, of the falling of the leaves from the trees, the coming of the frost, and the short, dark days. Now, partly perhaps because of my fear of cold and hunger, I noticed that no two days were the same, that as the year declined, there were changes of sky and stars and the behavior of birds that I had never known before.

Not, of course, that I was ever observant enough for Euny.

"What were the clouds like?" she asked, as ever, when I returned from an expedition. "Did the wind change? What birds did you see? Which trees have lost all their leaves? What shrubs still have flowers upon them? What was the moon like?"

It had been my habit to walk through the world in a pleasant dream, remembering stories or conversations, going back over bits of the past I had enjoyed, or having romantic fantasies about the future. Euny did not seem to understand this at all.

"You are hopeless, hopeless," she told me angrily. "You will never make a *doran*." I was wounded by this and sulkily tried to remember to notice the sort of things she asked about, but she had an unnerving way, after I had made a point of counting the birds or observing the clouds, of picking on something quite new—the shape of the landscape, the number of footpaths and the way they joined one another, the appearance of people we had met by the wayside, or animals. I tried harder, but it seemed to be no use at all.

In addition to hunger and cold I realized that I was also struggling with silence. Euny sometimes went all day without addressing a word to me. In desperation I had long conversations with Moon and with Borra, the pig, standing beside his sty and scratching his back with a stick. Euny often fed Borra scraps and sometimes I stole one or two of them for myself before giving them to him. He, after all, was very fat, whereas I was much thinner than I used to be. I enjoyed Borra's grunts, but I would rather have talked to another person.

"Do you ever feel lonely?" I asked Euny once. There was a long silence.

"Sometimes," she replied.

"Don't you mind?"

She made a gesture like pushing something away from her. "I am used to it. It doesn't matter."

When the chores were all done, Euny expected me to sit still as she did, she in her rocking chair, I on a cushion on the hearth. I hated doing this and soon learned to spin out the chores so that they kept me busy for much of the morning, but sooner or later there was nothing to do but to go back into the hut and sit down. Half a day would pass without conversation or movement. Sometimes I fell asleep—upright, since Euny saw no reason for me to lie down during the day. Always I yawned and fidgeted.

"It's very boring," I said unwarily once.

"Good," said Euny, and spoke no more. Not for the first time I hated her. I spent the time dreaming of food.

THERE WAS SOMETHING that I began to mind more than the cold and hunger. It was the feeling that while I was enduring all this discomfort and Euny's wounding sarcasm, I was learning nothing about the special sort of power that was the gift of the *doran*. I had supposed that Euny would sit me down and instruct me properly in the use of herbs and ointments, helping me to understand, as all my other teachers had done, instead of merely tossing off a comment about a plant now and then, but when I saw Euny working on her medicines and asked for information, she would wave me away with "It's not important," as if the whole thing were a secret, and suggest that it was time for me to get on with feeding the pig.

"How will I learn if you never teach me anything?" I asked crossly one day. She did not bother to reply.

9

THE WORST THING that ever happened in the first part of my stay with Euny was the day she spent a long time sharpening the big knife on a stone by the door and then offered it to me.

"Go on," she said to me, and I gazed at her in puzzlement.

"The pig," she said. "Kill it!"

I stared open-mouthed at her, looking from her face to the gleaming knife in her hand.

"I couldn't possibly," I said. I remembered the horrors of pig killing on the farms around Castle Dore—the squeals and the flowing blood. I had always shuddered and hurried by, back to the life of a princess.

"Someone has to do it!" said Euny. "So why not you?"

"Please don't make me," I begged her. (Already my experience of Euny should have taught me that this was the worst possible way of going about things.)

"I have noticed that you like to eat pig meat," Euny

said haughtily. "The old carcass is empty. If you don't kill this pig, there will be no meat for you to eat."

"You don't mean it!" I said. Fat bacon was most of our diet. I knew she did mean it. Furious with her, I snatched the knife out of her hand and went to the pigsty.

Borra had become a good friend of mine by now. At the sound of my footsteps he looked up expectantly. I hid the knife behind my back and talked kindly to him, noticing the life in the bright little eyes, the pleasure in his grunts. I went back to Euny.

"I can't do it!" I said, throwing down the knife. "It's cruel!"

"So we shall starve to death!" she said triumphantly, as if the prospect pleased her.

I tried to argue with her. "I don't understand. I thought the *doran*s loved the creatures of the world and wanted to care for them."

"What could show more love for an animal than eating it?" replied Euny.

"But you are taking its life away from it. All it has."

"For it to become part of the life in you. You are being false. What you will discover—*if* you ever stop being interested in yourself for long enough to notice the world around you—is that all life feeds off other life."

"But not Borra! He's so sweet, and I love him so much that I cannot kill him."

"But sweet or not you would eat him if I killed him. Is that not right?"

Shamefaced, I was forced to nod. I knew that I had only to smell bacon cooking to feel a wild hunger.

"So long as *you* don't have to feel responsible for killing him. So long as the princess does not get blood on her hands! Wonderful!"

Euny's scorn hurt me, but I minded it even more when she picked up the knife and handed it back to me.

"Hurry up! There is a lot of work to be done on the carcass, and we need to start while there is still plenty of daylight."

I left her again, but instead of going back to the sty I began to pace around the bottom of the tor. I had never been spoken to in my life in the way Euny spoke to me, and it left me helplessly angry. It was then that I noticed I was brandishing the knife furiously in the air—and suddenly I observed with a faint glimmer of unexpected amusement that what I was doing in my mind was plunging the knife into Euny. I couldn't kill a pig, but I had a secret longing, at least just for that moment, to kill her. Yet I knew that my future as a *doran* was linked to my obedience to Euny, that she would refuse to teach me if I did not do as she said. I paused outside Borra's pen, praying to his spirit to forgive me. This time I did not hide the knife, and he looked at it without fear. I held his head in one hand and with the other slipped the knife beneath his chin. My heart pounding, I pushed the knife against his throat. Immediately Borra began to struggle, and with tremendous force he threw me back against the wall. I had

not even cut him. Frightened now at the furious creature, I put the knife straight to his throat, shouting to
him, begging him at the top of my voice not to resist.
The knife made only the smallest cut, but suddenly
blood began to pour out of him and the knife itself was
slippery with it. Borra backed against the wall with
squeals that rang sickeningly through my head. I
wounded him again, but he was still full of fight and
began to come after me with his head lowered, making
a strange growling noise in his throat. For a while we
circled each other, Borra wanting to attack me but afraid
of the knife, me wanting to finish my terrible task but
afraid of his hoofs and his powerful snout. Desperate,
I lunged at him once more and knew from his scream
that I had hurt him, but also that this big angry animal
was now going to charge. I moved as quickly around
the little space of the pen as I could, until suddenly my
foot slipped in a puddle of blood. I fell. At that moment Borra also fell, and I could hear his dreadful la-
bored breathing as he lay on his side. Swiftly I stood
up, bent over him, and cut his windpipe properly. Although his legs twitched a bit, I knew he was within
seconds of death.

"Borra, forgive me," I said to him. "This was not my
choice."

White, shaking, covered in blood, I went back to the
hut. For a moment I was too upset to notice that Euny
was not alone, indeed that the hut seemed to be full of
people. There was my mother looking her most beautiful, her delicate pale face framed in a collar of fox.
There was Erith, shocked at the sight of me. There was

Gamal standing by the hearth regarding me sympathet-
ically and beside him another boy about our own age
who stared at me in open amusement. I stood there
looking mutely at them, bloodstained, my hair falling
over my face, the knife in my hand. My mother made
a small, stifled exclamation as she caught sight of me
and then was silent. Erith was less restrained.

"You look awful," she said.

"I've killed the pig," I said unnecessarily to Euny,
not knowing what else to say. Euny, quite unruffled by
the company, nodded with a small, pleased expression,
took the knife from me, and suggested that I should
change my smock. Gamal, trying to act as if all was as
usual, introduced me to Finbar, a new page at my father's court who had come to carry food and warm
clothes, which my mother and Erith had prepared for
me. Even in these circumstances I noticed that he was
a very handsome boy, with brilliant blue eyes and black
hair. As I tried to speak to my mother, Finbar, where
she could not see him, was pointing at me and silently
pretending to hold his sides with laughter, like a mocking jester behind the throne. I thought he was the rud-
est boy I had ever met.

LATER, MY HAIR COMBED and wearing a cleaner smock,
I walked with my mother to the foot of the strange-
shaped hill. A jumble of feelings fought inside me—
humiliation at being caught looking so dreadful, anger
at Euny for making me kill the pig, triumph at finally
having done it, apprehension about what my mother
would say. Would she persuade me to return to Castle

Dore? I realized I had very mixed feelings about that.

For a long time neither of us spoke.

"So how is it?" my mother said at last.

I started to mumble some reply but could not speak for the sob in my throat.

My mother stood for a long time looking up at the steep sides of the hill as if trying to read something from it. Then she said, "Of course you must come home if it is too dreadful. But I don't know; I have a feeling that you want to be here. Awful as it is."

An extraordinary surge of gratitude ran through me, gratitude that although she was my mother, she could see and understand something that went beyond my thinness, my swollen fingers, and my own anger and perplexity. I began to cry in earnest because of her love for me, and she put her arms around me.

"Why do I have to?" I asked her.

"I don't know."

"I felt so ashamed," I said, "that you and Erith and the boys saw me all bloodstained from killing the pig. And that Euny and I live in such poverty."

She lifted up her white profile and, looking like the daughter of a prince that she was, said, "You were always a brave child, Ninnoc. Knowing you, I expected you would live this ordeal with courage. Life with Euny is hard, but it won't go on forever." She smiled at me. "Don't despair."

"I don't understand it," I said, "but I seem to need to be here. And yet it *is* awful."

"One good thing," went on Erlain, "we have brought

you some food, some sacks of wheat and oats. That should help. That and the pig." She smiled at me again. "And Erith put in some blankets and pillows and a thick woolen cloak."

"Good," I said.

"Gamal has brought you some cakes and some wine. You should get a decent supper tonight."

"You do understand," I said in gratitude.

I was humbled by my mother's generosity, at her willingness to let me, her only child, follow a strange path. I flung my arms around her and this time we both wept.

I also had time to talk with Gamal.

"I shall come and see you sometimes," he said. "And so will Finbar. He's become a good friend. I'm teaching him our language—his home is on an island a long way north of England. He wants to be a navigator."

I felt a pang of jealousy at Gamal's transparent enthusiasm for his friend.

"I don't like Finbar," I said. "I think he is very rude."

"You'll like him when you know him better. Everybody likes him. He's awfully funny, and he's brave."

It was impossible to ignore Finbar completely when the party left. I held out my hand coldly to him, and he kissed it, as was the custom, still taunting, it seemed to me, with mocking eyes.

"I hope *you* will come again, Gamal," I said pointedly.

I FELT very lonely when they had all gone away and I was back alone with Euny again, but I had no time to dwell on it since Euny and I spent the rest of the day cutting up the pig—a tiring, messy business—so that it could be salted. We did cook some of it at once, though, and had a marvelous supper, which I ate ravenously.

"We won't starve this winter," said Euny with satisfaction, looking at the sacks stored in the corner of the hut.

"What did you do in other winters?" I asked curiously.

"Survived," said Euny shortly.

"The trouble with being hungry or cold," I said thoughtfully, "is that you think of nothing else. It's like having a pain. On the other hand, you really appreciate it when there is food to eat or a warm fire. I never knew food to taste as good as it has these last few weeks."

Euny grunted.

"I didn't know I could kill anything," I said, still minding about Borra, even though he tasted very good.

Euny smiled a wrinkled, leathery smile that I had never seen before.

"You were a good, obedient girl," she said.

"You didn't give me much choice," I replied crossly.

"I am proud of you," she said, and I could scarcely believe my ears.

10

ONE DAY Euny said, "Tomorrow we go to see Angharad of the West."

"Who is she? Where does she live?"

"A long journey. You'll see."

"But suppose Gamal comes to see me while I'm gone."

"He'll just have to go home again, won't he?"

IT WAS a bright winter day when the two of us set off, with the sun winking on icy puddles and the sky blue and clear. The air seemed to sparkle. The prospect of a change had cheered me and I felt happier than I had for some time, even though Euny insisted on walking extremely fast. By now Moon was too big to fit in even the largest pocket, and I carried him in a special bag I had made for him out of an old shift.

My warm cloak was very comforting, but my boots felt too small for my swollen toes, and I could feel the cold of the ground through the soles as they slipped and slithered. My hands quickly became blue and numb, and even with an old ragged blanket of Euny's around my head and shoulders I could feel the wind biting me. Euny, as usual, seemed not to notice the cold at all.

"Don't dawdle, girl," she said whenever I paused for breath. We had not brought much food with us, just some bread and some withered apples.

Much later we stopped at a farm and Euny begged some milk. The farmer's wife was baking hot rolls and the air was filled with the delicious smell of new bread. She picked out two rolls each and gave them to us. Seeing my wan face and frozen hands, she asked us in to rest before the fire and then suggested that it was too late to go on that night and that there was hay enough in the barn to keep us warm. I slept well that night in deep gratitude for her kindness, though Euny roused me from a sound sleep before it was light and insisted that we must be on our way. Rosy from the nest of hay, my chilblains itching at the unaccustomed warmth, I stumbled out yawning, ate my second roll and drank the rest of the milk, and we set off again.

On this day we walked along a huge sea channel, a giant estuary like a sea itself. From the cliffs we could see dangerous rocks below—ships stayed well out in the center. The blue-gray color of the sea was shot with white, like a ripped garment with its lining showing through.

Sustained by a good night's sleep and a breakfast, I found that I walked faster and incurred fewer rebukes from Euny, though the endless questions about what I had seen on the walk—"How many ships?" and so on—continued. She had spoiled the pleasure of walking for me, filling it with anxieties about noticing and remembering. I did seem to be a little better at it than I had been, however.

By that evening, to my distress, we were miles from any human habitation. We drank water from a stream, but we had nothing to eat, and I was bitterly hungry. When it grew too dark and I was too tired for us to walk any farther, we sat on a log in a wood and simply waited for the night to pass. I took Moon from his traveling bag and watched with envy as he swooped over the moorland in search of food.

"I'm hungry," I said accusingly. And then when no reply was forthcoming, "Why didn't we prepare properly for this journey? We could have brought more bread with us, maybe some beer."

"But then you miss the pleasure," said Euny.

"What pleasure?"

"Of living as birds do from the hand of nature."

I thought of the starved birds I had often found lying dead on the ground in winter.

"Birds often die at the hand of nature."

"Sometimes. Mostly not."

I listened to the ravening eagle inside me demanding to be fed.

"I must have food," I said desperately.

"If there is no food, you simply have to be hungry."

"Don't you mind being hungry?"

Euny hesitated.

"Nowadays, not at all. It is like the weather—I live

with it. But when I was a child . . . yes, I wept a great deal about being hungry."

I was intrigued. Euny had never before told me anything about her past—I am not sure that I thought she had one, that she had not emerged into the world full-grown, wearing her greeny-black clothes. I hoped she would say more, but she did not, and I did not dare to press her.

"Tell me where we are going," I asked at last to distract myself from all my discomforts.

"To one of the greatest *doran*s in the land. This country, you know, has many women of power, but Angharad is one of great power, and she has offered to teach you."

"What sort of power will I have?"

"The mending sort, the healing kind," Euny said shortly and crossly. *"If* you are ever ready for it. *When* you can use it rightly."

That night seemed interminably long, and it was dreadful to have to set off walking again. My feet were now so swollen that I could only hobble along with difficulty. My hunger had mysteriously vanished, as it does when no food is in prospect, though I felt quite weak and occasionally a little faint. We paused only once to drink water from a spring.

Then in the late afternoon we breasted a hill overlooking the sea, and Euny pointed to a little house set in the valley, with the sparkling waters of a lake behind it. Smoke was rising from the smoke hole, and there was something about the house that was pleasing and reassuring. I quickened my painful steps.

When we got nearer I could see something bright-colored hanging over the wall of a storehouse. There were patches of vivid red and yellow and green, but I was almost too tired to wonder about them, still less to ask questions.

It took us a while longer to reach the house, and by the time we did it was nearly dark. Euny lifted the latch and we entered a shadowy fire-lit room in which Angharad, a woman of graceful middle age, rose to greet us. The large fire made the room deliciously warm. There was the scent of a rich, meaty stew in the air.

I unwrapped the blanket from my head and stood uncertainly in the soft firelight, feeling as if I might burst into tears. The room swirled disturbingly about me just when I wanted so much to look at it. I had a horrible feeling that I was going to be sick, and then I was aware of Angharad catching me as I fell.

When I came to from my faint, Angharad was very gently easing the boots from my swollen feet.

"When did you last eat?" she was asking Euny.

I was aware at once of the comfort and refinement of life in Angharad's house and felt ashamed of my dirty clothes and ragged blanket. But Angharad showed no sign of despising us. When I felt better it was lovely to be drawn forward to the fire—though the heat caused my toes to itch furiously—to sit in a comfortable chair and fill my hungry stomach (my appetite had sprung back to life at the first sniff of the stew).

There was a sort of step with cushions on it around the hearth, and a big chair. In one corner stood a loom strung in brilliant colors, and in another corner a ladder passed up into a shadowy chamber. The chair, the table, and the cushions were covered in bright fabric, in the palest pink, rosy orange, a deep inky blue, all of them glowing like jewels in the half-dark of the firelight. The color, the comfort, and the rich taste of the stew could not have been more different from the hardships of Euny's hut. There was also a smell of roses, one that, I would later know, seemed to pervade Angharad's house. To this day I can never smell a rose without remembering her.

Angharad, wearing a pretty red gown, with her shining fair hair and her gentle apple-cheeked face, was not in the least like Euny. She reminded me a little of my mother, and I was instantly drawn to her. While she talked to Euny—a conversation about people who were unknown to me—I was aware of her readiness to include me, the way her gray eyes turned to me and smiled with a sympathy to which I had grown unaccustomed. At the same time her hands were busy with her spindle. Gradually I grew warmer and relaxed on my cushion, but was immediately aware of a desperate need to sleep. Suddenly Angharad interrupted the conversation with Euny and stood up.

"Come!" she said to me. "You are tired out."

She picked up a candleholder, lit a candle from the fire, and led the way up the ladder. Above were two chambers, a big one and a small one. She took me to the small one, where there were two beds upon the floor, straw-filled pallets covered with bright-colored blankets, and pointed to the one that had a thin white sleeping shift folded on it. She left me and I undressed, settled Moon comfortably on a beam, and crept into the nest of rustling straw. Then Angharad came back carrying bandages and a jar of ointment. She tended the open sores on my feet. Then she tucked the blankets around me and kissed me gently.

"I hope you'll be very happy in my house!" she said. Then the waves of sleep were lapping around me.

11

I WAS WOKEN by a voice saying insistently, *"Please wake up. I want to talk to you."* With a start I came to, saw sunlight brilliant on the white walls of the room, and could not think where I was. I turned my head and saw a girl about my own age, a very pretty girl sitting cross-legged by the bed, watching me intently. She had long fair hair, braided, falling down over her shoulders, and her eyes were a vivid green.

"Who are you?" I asked in surprise.

"Trewyn," she said. "I live with Angharad. I'm a sort of apprentice. Didn't they tell you about me?"

It seemed useless to explain that Euny never told me anything, so I simply smiled at her.

"I'm longing to talk to you," she said, full of eagerness. "Angharad said you were a princess!"

I must confess that I felt pleased that Trewyn was obviously impressed by this, but I still felt too shy to launch into a long description of my life.

"Do you sleep in here too?" I asked, seeing the other bed disarranged.

"Yes. It *is* going to be nice having you. I was longing to wake you up and talk to you when I got home last night. I was out looking for a plant Angharad needed to make a dye. But she wouldn't let me wake you up." Trewyn paused for a moment. "Are you hungry?"

I nodded. She got up and went out of the room, and for a moment I caught sight of her lovely profile and long neck—it was she, not I, who looked like a princess, I thought. I lay back, propped on my pillow, still quite tired but enjoying the warmth of my bed, the simple lines of the room, and the fact that for the first time in months I was to have a companion of my own age.

In a little while Trewyn was back with an oatcake and a drink they make in those parts by fermenting the whey of milk. The good plain taste of the oatcake— delicious like all Angharad's cooking—and the fiery warmth of the drink put new energy into me. While I ate, Trewyn asked about Moon and tried to talk to him, but he blinked stupidly at her.

I climbed down the ladder to the room where the two *doran*s were sitting in front of the fire together. Euny, usually so pale, looked a little flushed from the fire. She looked up at me, saying, "Tomorrow I will travel north. I will be gone for two months. Angharad will teach you in that time." The pleasure must have shown in my face, because she said rather crossly, "I hope she won't spoil you too much."

"Nonsense!" said Angharad. "She's a sensible girl, and she and Trewyn will be company for each other. Come back and fetch her in the spring."

I THINK my obvious preference for Angharad must have rankled Euny. The next day I walked a little way with her on her journey. Then she stopped.

"Go back now." She hesitated. "You think I am hard on you, maybe that I do not care about you. I can only be a *doran* in the way that is natural for me." Euny waited, as if she were trying to say more but could not manage it. Then she kissed me roughly on the cheek, turned, and marched away. I was touched by her speech but could not wait to get back to Angharad and Trewyn.

One of the reasons that Angharad had offered to keep me for a while, I think now, was that she believed Euny was starving me and wanted to feed me up. The food was generous and delicious, and she encouraged me to enjoy it, occasionally saying things like, "Young girls need proper nourishment," which I took to be an oblique criticism of Euny. Not that I felt she disliked Euny.

"You have one of the most remarkable *doran*s in the country as your teacher," Angharad said to me one day, when she and I were out gathering docks to make a green dye.

"How do you mean?" I asked with bitterness. "What is it that is so remarkable?"

"Among the *doran*s we speak of people having power, you know. We don't mean power like kings or popes have power, of course, but power to bring things back into a sort of harmony, like tuning an instrument that's gone flat."

"And Euny can do that?" I said disbelievingly.

"In a most unusual way, yes. She sees to the heart of things."

There was something I wanted to say to Angharad, only it was difficult because it felt disloyal.

"She's very hard on me."

Angharad was silent for a long while, and then she said, "Did Euny ever tell you the story of her life?" I shook my head.

"When Euny was a tiny little girl her parents were killed in a raid. Some of the tribes were very brutal in those days. They didn't just take cattle and crops. . . . Some say Euny's mother was killed in front of her—that she escaped only because she was hidden in the roof of the barn but that she peeked out and saw what happened. Two or three of the children were left, but their house was destroyed and they had nowhere to go. They lived as they could, roaming the countryside, orphaned and homeless, begging food or work here and there, sleeping wherever they could be warm. Euny's whole childhood was like that. Only when she was fourteen, a famous *doran* called Phrene took Euny in. She was starved and sick like a little wild animal in winter, but Phrene was very gentle with her, and slowly Euny became strong and well. I know this"—Angharad gave me her sweet smile—"because I was Phrene's apprentice, and Euny and I were sister *doran*s-in-training, just like you and Trewyn are. Phrene reckoned," she went on, "that Euny was the best pupil she ever had, and as you know, good *doran*s are made by good teachers. You will be a good—perhaps great—*doran* partly because Euny trained you."

"But she *doesn't* train me," I said obstinately, although I was very moved by this tragic story.

"Child," said Angharad slowly, and there was a long pause, "open your eyes."

WHEN WE were back in the house, we boiled a vat of the dock leaves with vinegar, and I pushed skeins of white wool into it.

"Without the vinegar—what is called the mordant," Angharad said, "the dye would run as soon as you washed the wool. It is the biting acid that makes the color fast. It was brave of you to leave home to go and live with Euny. I know what Euny's housekeeping is like. You must often have been frozen as well as hungry."

The pleasure of Angharad's sympathy made it possible to swallow my resentment.

"It was rather cold," I admitted. "But I wasn't really brave. I just couldn't help myself. Also I know that Euny has something to teach me . . . if she only would."

Angharad turned and looked at me. "Perhaps you think learning to be a *doran* is like learning French or mathematics. But it isn't. It's quite different."

"But I've only got a year and a day," I reminded her, "and so far I haven't learned anything."

"Well, after today you will have learned how to dye wool with dock leaves."

Later, when we fished the shining green skeins out of the vat and hung them over the storehouse wall to dry in the sun, I had a sense of achievement but thought, "It's nothing to do with being a *doran*."

Although Angharad fed me properly and kept me warm, she expected me to work hard. To begin with she taught me how to tease wool, the process of preparing it for spinning. I learned to pull the wool off the fleece, take out the dirty and tangled bits, part the wool between my fingers until it was of even texture, and then comb it into delicate little rolls.

"It's the preparation that counts in spinning," Angharad said. "If you are lazy about that, you will never spin an even thread."

Then she showed me how to knot some thread onto the spindle and, spinning it between my feet, twist the combed wool onto it while the spindle revolved. It was very difficult at first because the thread kept breaking and going into lumps. It was nothing like the perfect, even thread that Angharad made so rhythmically. I persisted though, and eventually, to my great pride, a cone of spun wool rested on the spindle. Then, instead of letting me whirl the spindle between my feet, she stood a spinning dish on the floor beside me, and I found I could spin much faster and more easily than before. I was delighted at first, then I got bored and began to spin more carelessly, wanting to be done with it. The result was rather poor. Angharad did not scold me. She simply expected that I would go on practicing.

"Wool is a living thing," she said once. "That is why you cannot spin wool from a dead sheep."

Watching her spin, I noticed how as she joined one piece of wool to another the little hairs of the wool clung together to make a strong thread with no trace of a join. As we teased the wool plucked from the fleece,

I suddenly saw it with new eyes, noticing the tiny black flecks of peat in it and the yellow waxy substance that made my hands soft. As we carded it and made it into long webs of wool, I felt its softness, its delicate strength. Angharad's long slim fingers twirling the distaff and making a fine even thread made it seem almost as if she spun it out of herself. I caught myself trying to match her rhythm, to move into the kind of easy concentration that produced a thread without lumps, but I kept finding that either I tensed myself and squeezed the unspun wool so hard that it would not flow properly into the thread or that I pulled the threads out so far that they thinned and broke. It was more difficult than I had thought at first.

"It's how you feel, isn't it?" I said to Angharad one day in a moment of insight. "That's what makes the evenness of the thread. You need to concentrate yet not notice that you're concentrating." I suddenly remembered what she had said about learning to be a *doran* being different from learning French.

"Do you think spinning could be helpful in learning how to be a *doran?*" I asked.

Angharad laughed. "It's exactly the same thing," she said.

I frowned.

"How can it be the same thing? Every old woman sitting spinning on her doorstep knows how to do this. They're not all *doran*s?"

"No, not all, but don't underestimate their wisdom. When you are wise it won't make them stupid."

12

GRADUALLY ANGHARAD taught me to dye with many different plants—with leaves and roots and berries. On almost every sunny day the wall was hung with wool in jewel colors—the pink, orange, and red of madder and lichen, the blue and purple of woad, the yellow of dandelions, marsh marigolds, and heather, each carefully set with its mordant. When I looked at the wool dyed a wonderful delicate yellow from lichen, I remembered with amusement the frustrating morning I had spent trying to collect urine from Betsy the goat—goat's urine being the best mordant for lichen.

Mornings were spent cleaning the house, drawing water, building a fire, preparing food, finding herbs, making and using dyes. In the afternoons the three of us sat down to our spinning, often whiling away the time with stories and songs. Trewyn and I would have an hour or two to ourselves in the late afternoon, and then after supper we returned to our spinning.

"When you have enough wool," Angharad said to me, "I shall teach you to weave."

"What shall I weave?" I asked her.

Angharad nodded to Trewyn, who left the room and came back with a cloak over her arm. At a further signal from Angharad, Trewyn put the cloak on over her simple brown smock and fastened it with a gold clasp. The cloak was a deep dark green, lit here and there with a vivid flash of pink, a fish or a flower that floated in its dusky depths. Trewyn's slim body, long neck, and beautiful profile with its perfect cheekbones seemed to take on dignity and mystery. Somehow the cloak seemed to reveal everything about her that I already knew as well as other things about her that I had only guessed at.

"This is the cloak of a *doran*," said Angharad. "Every *doran* has one, and it needs to be carefully made because one day it will be your protection against the magic of sorcerers. It must be as perfect as it can be."

"Will mine be like that?" I asked, amazed that Angharad might think me capable of making such a cloak.

"No. Your cloak will be as you make it. When you thread the loom, you will know which colors to use. That is why you need to prepare a good stock of colors now, so that you will have what you need."

I RETURNED to my spinning with a new zeal, determined now to make the thread as perfect as I could. It reflected my mood continually. It broke when I was tired or angry or impatient and flowed effortlessly when

I was calm and happy. Angharad gave me a shelf to store the wool for my cloak, and every day I added to the colored skeins.

It was a real relief to me that I was no longer cold or hungry. Even when the sleeping chamber grew cold on the frostiest nights, it was always possible to creep down and sit by the dying embers of the fire. And there was always enough food, though it was simple—milk and goat cheese, porridge, bread, beer. I was no longer tortured by chilblains, nor weary from hunger. It felt like a very precious sort of freedom.

One day Angharad said to me, "It is time to start weaving now. You must choose the threads with which to make the warp of your cloth."

I looked helplessly at the shelf with its many colored skeins and balls of wool.

"I don't know how to choose," I said lamely.

"Look inside yourself," Angharad said. "You do know really."

I looked inside myself but no knowledge came, only a sort of panic.

"I don't know," I said again. "You choose."

Angharad did not reply, but began moving around the house, preparing supper. Trewyn was out on some errand of her own. Moon stared down at me from the beam above my head, at a time when he was usually out hunting for food. I sat feeling bewildered at what was expected of me, and when supper came I was grateful for the diversion.

After supper, I turned to pick up my spindle, but Angharad shook her head.

"Weaving," she said emphatically. I continued to sit

on my stool, feeling silly. Much later Angharad and
Trewyn rose to go to bed. Angharad looked at me, her
gentle motherly face unexpectedly determined.

"No point in going to bed till you've solved it," she
said. Trewyn threw me a sympathetic glance as the two
of them left me there.

When they had gone I straightened my aching back
and wondered what to do. I could, of course, sleep in
Angharad's chair and she would be none the wiser, but
this would bring me no closer to solving my problem.
I looked again at the wool on the shelf and felt more
puzzled than ever. I stared at each color in turn—the
pinks, the reds, the oranges, the blues, the purples, the
yellows, the browns, the greens—and tried to imagine
beginning work with them, but none of them claimed
me.

I wiped away a tear. I could see that I would still be
sitting here at breakfast time and that even Angharad,
who was always kind, would sternly force me to wait
until inspiration struck. I could, of course, just take up
whichever color came to hand and start work with that.
Angharad would not know (or would she?) that I had
cheated. Exasperated, as my hand hovered over the shelf,
I thought that I might choose one of the colors blind-
folded.

Yet immediately my hand fell back to my side.
However tired I was, however hopeless it seemed, there
was simply no point in cheating. If this cloak was
somehow to be my protection, it needed to be woven
with truth. Both Euny and Angharad, so very different
from each other, had taught me that.

For a few moments I felt lonely and rather cross, as if someone ought to be telling me what to do. The feeling of crossness grew and grew until I slapped the side of the loom in rage. Why didn't my teachers help me? Almost at once I saw the answer. It was that like a small child taking its first steps, there was something I needed to try out, something only I could teach myself.

Now I was very still, trying to notice something in myself that I had never noticed before. Sweating a little, with a sense of growing excitement and trembling a little too, I heard myself suddenly say out loud, "Who are you?" And then, quite firmly, as if I had never properly understood this before, I answered myself, "You are Juniper." As I said this, my hand, completely sure of itself, reached out and picked up wool of the deepest midnight blue and luminous gray-blue. My hand reached out again and this time it took up white undyed wool. On its third journey to the shelf it chose two yellowy colors—a deep amber and a lighter yellow. Did I really know that these were the "right" colors? Yes, I did, but I did not know how I knew. I began reaching the midnight-blue wool around the loom, knotting it, weighting it, too concentrated on what I was doing to find it odd that it was now the middle of the night. At one point, however, I looked up and saw that Moon's amber eyes were still fixed unwinkingly upon me. When Angharad got up to milk Betsy the next morning, there were many threads on the loom. She came straight across the room to look, nodded with pleasure, and said, "You got it right. I knew you would."

13

DO YOU *want* to be a *doran?*" I remember Trewyn asking me one day as we sat high on the branch of a tree.

"I want to *understand* all kinds of things," I said. "Maybe more than some people do. Or maybe they do it differently. And I don't want to be pushed into getting married just for the sake of it."

"I'm a bit scared about being a *doran*," Trewyn admitted. "Angharad can do real magic, you know, though she doesn't bother very often."

"Yes, I think Euny can too," I said. "I suppose that means that eventually we will do magic."

"I used to think when I was little that it would be lovely to do magic—imagine being able to fly or get the house to clean itself up all on its own, or have something good to eat just when you felt like it."

"Or get to a place quickly without having to walk all the way," I said.

"Now I'm not so sure," said Trewyn. "Exciting in a way, but maybe something I'd rather not meddle with. I mean, I like to feel that you can *depend* on things being predictable—apples falling downward, a bowl of porridge being empty when it *is* empty, people being there or not being there."

Trewyn was silent for a while. Then she began to tell me of an extraordinary experience.

"I went to Caerleon on an errand for Angharad one morning," she began, "and on the road I met a terrifying dog. It was very big—the biggest dog I had ever seen—black, with great teeth, a slavering tongue, and a strange smell. It would not let me move. Every time I took a step forward it growled and looked as if it would attack me, but when I started walking slowly backward the way I had come, the same thing happened. I stood there until noon, too frightened to move. Then it was as if I talked to Angharad inside myself, asking her what I should do. Suddenly there she was, right beside me on the road, though she did not look at me or talk to me. She spoke to the dog in a language I did not understand. Then she took me by the hand and led me right past it. I turned around to see what the dog was doing, but it had disappeared. When I turned back, Angharad had disappeared too.

"When I got home I asked her about it, of course. I half hoped she would deny it, say it had all been my imagination, but she simply nodded her head and said, 'You needed help.' Then, and this was the worst bit, she added, 'That was no ordinary dog.'

" 'It was bigger than any dog I ever saw,' I agreed.

" 'I mean—it wasn't a dog at all,' Angharad said. 'I have a great enemy in Caerleon. I supposed he was away and that it was safe to send you. But I was mistaken. He had returned to Caerleon and he recognized you as being my apprentice.'

" 'How could he recognize me?' I asked. 'He had never seen me.'

" 'Sorcerers recognize anything or anyone that belongs to a *doran*—their clothes, their animals, or their apprentices.'

" 'How?' I asked, and I could not believe Angharad's answer. 'By their *smell*,' she said."

I was struck by this story of Trewyn's. I was also trying to see if I could smell Trewyn or remember whether any special smell came from Angharad. Yes, I thought, she smelled of roses. Euny's house certainly had a distinctive smell—damp and musty—and her person also had a smell—of garlic, and spice, and of unwashed skin—but I didn't smell like that. Or at least I hoped I didn't.

"Somehow," Trewyn finished, "that whole episode scared me. Up till then I thought magic was exciting, but then I knew that there was real danger."

"What danger?"

"That sorcerers could kill you or enslave you. They can take the spirit out of you, you know—they call it ghosting—and you wander around not knowing who you are. Sometimes now I just want to go back home and lead an ordinary life and not get mixed up in magic."

Finally, hesitantly, I told Trewyn about the time I had done some magic myself—how I had healed Gamal.

Yet when later I had tried to cure my own chilblains, it had not worked.

"Do you think it just works when you do it for other people?" asked Trewyn. "I mean, I've never seen Angharad use magic to make her own life easier—to save bothering to grind any more meal, say, or to avoid the labor of threading up a loom."

PERHAPS THE TALK of magic influenced me in some way. A few days before, Angharad had been showing me how to weave, and that afternoon, standing alone at the big loom while the other two were out somewhere, I had the strangest feeling that the feathery white figures I was weaving into the midnight-blue background were three-dimensional, that they were just as solidly part of the world as the stool or the loom itself. Later, when I took up the spindle, I felt as if the thread was flowing not just from the puff of wool hanging over my left shoulder, but through my arm and indeed through my whole body. For the first time the thread was perfectly even. It looked like the thread that Angharad spun, and what was more, I knew that I was spinning somewhat as Angharad did, in an effortless rhythm.

When Angharad came back, she looked at the weaving I had done and at the thread I had spun.

"So!" she said. "You are ready!"

"Ready for what?" I asked.

"You must work hard at your cloak. Euny will be back soon."

As so often, that day when it all seemed so easy was

followed by one in which it all seemed impossibly difficult. I realized that I had made a slight mistake in following the pattern of my weaving, but it was a long way back and I simply couldn't be bothered to undo it. In any case, the error was so tiny that it scarcely showed at all.

"WHAT DID Angharad mean, 'ready'?" I asked Trewyn in our white and timber sleeping chamber. "Ready for what?"

Trewyn's lovely face looked troubled.

"I don't know," she said. "Some sort of ceremony, maybe. Or an ordeal—*doran*s are said to train their apprentices with ordeals."

"What do you mean?" I asked, uneasy now myself.

"They want to find out if you are strong enough, brave enough," she said.

"But Angharad and Euny wouldn't do anything really *cruel* to us, would they?" I asked.

"They might if they thought it would be good for us," Trewyn replied gloomily.

I often thought about this conversation in the days that followed, as I finished the rich material of my cloak. Yet I would look across the room at Angharad's kind motherly face, and I could not believe that she wished me any ill. And even Euny, hard as life with her had been, had never set out to hurt or frighten me—she was just not very good at imagining what I was feeling. I felt that I trusted both *doran*s.

Trewyn, however, felt far less confident than I did. She was plainly frightened of the coming ordeal—

whatever it was—and she began to sleep badly. Occasionally she would wake me with her tossing and turning. Twice she had bad dreams and began to shout in her sleep. In the morning she was pale and heavy-eyed. I saw Angharad look thoughtfully at her, and I wondered if she would give her a word of comfort, but she did not.

Angharad spoke only once about what was to come, on the day we cut the heavy material from the loom. Joyful that my long task was done, I picked up the material and draped it for a moment around my shoulders. It was very heavy. Angharad glanced at me, then lowered her eyes as if she had seen more than she wanted to see.

"Take it off," she said quite sharply. "It is not time."

"When will it be time?" I inquired.

"There will be a . . . ceremony," she said. "For you and Trewyn. When Euny returns."

"What will it be like?"

"I cannot tell you."

"Trewyn is very scared about it," I said disloyally, wanting a little comfort myself.

"I know," Angharad said, and turned to poke the fire. I was not reassured.

THERE WAS STILL a lot of work to be done on the cloak. From the wooden chest Angharad produced a bolt of dusky orange silk for the lining. She also gave me two topaz stones set in silver with which to make a clasp. And finally I had to embroider a collar for it. I spent several days drawing patterns on a piece of slate, until one pattern—a design that grew unexpectedly from the look of Moon's claws—seemed exactly right to me. Angharad gave me some seed pearls to sew into the pattern, and they represented claws very convincingly.

"This will be the most precious thing you will ever own," she said, "and you will keep it all your life."

ON THE DAY that I sewed the last stitch of my cloak and Angharad folded it safely away for me in the big chest, Euny came back. It was a raw March day with a bitter east wind cutting across the moor, and Trewyn and I were glad to come home from our walk, back to the fire and a hot drink. And there was Euny, sitting on the hearth as if she had never been away.

14

ONCE OR TWICE on my walks with Trewyn I had noticed an odd-shaped building near the circle of standing stones where she often liked to go and sit. It was made of stone with curving walls that bent upward toward the ridge of the roof. The line of the ridge, I had noticed once, pointed to the center of the stone circle. One day, when rain was pelting down, we had pushed open the creaking wooden door and gone inside. It was much bigger than it appeared from the outside, with a plain earth floor that looked as if it had been recently raked and a center hearth with a fire already laid upon it. We could see this only by leaving the door open since there were no slits or holes in the walls to give light.

"Someone uses this place," I remarked to Trewyn. "But who? And for what?" She made some reply about it being a shepherd's hut, but I knew what they looked like—tiny rudely constructed wooden buildings with just

room for a man to curl up and sleep out of the wind
and the rain. Not like this at all.

Back at home I noticed that Angharad was no longer
pushing us to continual spinning and weaving—she gave
us time to idle the day away as she had never done
before. She and Euny were often deep in conversation—not always agreeing, I suspect—the sort of conversation that breaks off as soon as you come into the
room.

"Something funny's going on," I said to Trewyn.

"It's the ceremony," she replied anxiously. "They are
getting us ready for it."

One April afternoon they called us in. We had been
punting on the lake on a raft we had laboriously nailed
together. Trewyn had pondweed clinging around one
leg from pushing the raft out with me on it, and her
clothes were wringing wet. I was scarcely looking better. I had torn my smock, and my hair was wild and
knotted from blowing in the wind. We were a dreadful
sight.

"You must both be bathed," Angharad said, and I
could see enormous cauldrons of water already steam-
ing on the fire. "Wash every part of yourselves, including your hair."

We took turns using the tub and washing each other's backs. I could feel Trewyn's hands trembling as she
said to me in a quiet voice, "It's going to happen." Certainly there did seem to be something odd going on.
When we got out of the tub, we were each given a big
cloth on which to dry ourselves. There was no sign of
clean clothes.

"Shall I go up and get a clean smock?" I asked at last.

Instead of replying Angharad simply handed me a huge sheet, and she gave another to Trewyn.

We were combing out our wet hair in front of the fire when I said, "Is supper going to be soon?"

"You are fasting," said Euny.

"We are all fasting," Angharad amended.

Trewyn and I exchanged nervous glances.

"Why?" Trewyn finally croaked out.

Angharad shook her head as if she could not answer, and Euny looked out the door as she had done several times already. It was dark outside, and a wind was blowing, whining ominously around Angharad's house. I wished that if something frightening had to happen to us, it could happen on some other night, or better yet, by day. Trewyn and I had already speculated on every possibility—would they beat us or torture us? Make us eat or drink horrible substances? Both of us were sure we had heard stories of such things. We sat by the fire, two substantial ghosts, and after a bit a full moon, huge and brilliant, appeared in the sky. Euny nodded to Angharad. "Time to go," she said.

They stood up, took the sheets from us, and said, "We are going out."

"Where are our clothes?" asked Trewyn, her slim body tense with distress.

"No clothes," said Angharad. "You will go just like that."

"I can't," Trewyn wailed. "We might meet someone."

"We won't meet anyone," said Euny definitely. "Come along. There is work to be done."

Trewyn threw an agonized glance in my direction, hoping, perhaps, that I would join her in a rebellion. For some reason I was less fearful than she. I simply followed Angharad and Euny to the door. Once outside the stones hurt my feet, the wind, which was cold, blew painfully on my bare flesh, and quite soon my teeth were chattering. Even the soft tickle of my loose hair on my bare shoulders felt unfamiliar. What were we doing? And why? The moon, a huge yellow disk at the end of the path we were following, lit the landscape in precise lines without shadow. Trewyn's trembling naked body in front of me shone in a gold light.

Only when we reached the stone hut did I realize that that was where we were heading. It was a relief to march our cold bodies out of the bitter wind, though the only place on which to sit was a cold stone. There was an unlit fire laid on the center hearth and two big piles of wood beside it. I looked wistfully at it, my body shaking and shuddering with cold.

The four of us sat down and Angharad and Euny lit a rush lamp and began reciting, by heart, a long and very tedious poem. It spoke of dead heroes and heroines, most of whom I had never heard of; it was a recital of the interminable history of the *doran*s, whose wisdom had been frequently persecuted. At the end the words began to be addressed to me and Trewyn, admonitions that we should be worthy of our high calling, should enter into harmony with the world, should care for others, should never work magic for our own aggrandizement.

Then Euny bade us to lie facedown full-length upon the ground.

"Think before you answer these questions," she told us. "Do you wish to be admitted to the order of *doran?*" she wanted to know.

Lying shivering on the cold ground, I wished that I were safely home in bed. If this was what being a *doran* was all about, it was hard to see why anyone would wish to be one. Yet when I thought of the hazel tree, of the strange way that Euny and I had come together, and of my experiences at Angharad's house as I wove the cloth for my cloak, I knew that life was pushing me toward the particular sort of wisdom that Euny and Angharad had. I felt that I had no real choice.

"I wish to become a *doran,*" I said through chattering teeth.

I waited for Trewyn to make a similar declaration, but she lay in silence.

"Trewyn?" Angharad asked at last.

"I don't know," Trewyn wailed. "I'm frightened."

I could hear Angharad and Euny conferring.

"Very well," Angharad said finally. "We will continue with the ritual. At the end of it, Trewyn, we will ask you the question again, and if then you answer no, you will leave us and never mention to anyone what you have seen here."

One of them had touched a light to the fire on the hearth and I could hear twigs crackling.

"You may get up and come to the fire," Euny said to us, and we sat on our haunches beside it. Trewyn was weeping, whereas I felt a kind of sullen anger.

Euny took a handful of herbs from a bowl on the ground and began to chew them. Then she passed the bowl to Angharad, who followed her example.

I was surprised to see Euny now piling green wood on the fire, when there was a perfectly good supply of dry wood. Inevitably, the stone hut quickly filled with acrid smoke. My eyes brimmed with tears, I began to cough convulsively, and for a few moments I lost sight of the others in the smoke. Feeling that I was suffocating, I made for the door but found that I could not open it. To my surprise, it appeared to be bolted from the outside.

Groping my way back in the smoke, I bumped into Trewyn and we sat with our arms around each other, still shaking with cold, as far from the fire as we could get. Then the smoke cleared a little, and to our astonishment Angharad and Euny had disappeared!

I noticed that the green wood had been placed in a separate pile, and I had no doubt that the two *dorans* had deliberately filled the hut with smoke. But there was another huge pile of dry wood next to it, and I put two large logs on the fire. Trewyn crept back to the hearth, still coughing.

"Why did they do it?" she asked. "Is it part of the test?"

I was so angry at being locked in the hut that I could scarcely speak.

"You do suppose they intend to come back?" Trewyn asked tremulously. "They wouldn't just leave us here?"

"Of course they'll come back," I said with a confidence that was not entirely real. Suppose the two of us were destined to be some sort of sacrifice? Suppose they were going to leave us to starve?

I noticed a shabby wooden chest in the far corner of the hut and dragged it closer to the fire. For a while Trewyn and I sat on it—it was warmer than the cold stones—then slid down to the earth floor and sat leaning against each other, propped up by the chest, our feet comfortably toasting by the fire. Its flames now burned in a deep old-rose color shot through at moments with vivid blue. There was a sweet smell so pure and fragrant that for a moment I almost forgot where I was. I closed my eyes to enjoy it and when I opened them again, everything seemed a little bigger and clearer, as if I could suddenly see better.

"Do you see anything?" Trewyn asked hesitatingly after a while.

"Not exactly. Things just look more beautiful. I think the smoke must be magic. And I feel a lot warmer."

Even as I spoke, I noticed the grain in the wooden door as the firelight flickered over it. It looked like the markings on a snake's back, and like a snake, it moved. I did not feel threatened, simply delighted at the beauty of the design.

"The door!" I said to Trewyn.

"Snakes!" she said cheerfully, and I felt full of love for her that she could share this vision with me. I now

noticed that the stones on the walls shone with a sort
of golden light. The shadows between them were deep
and lustrous, and there were faces—not ugly or frightening faces as sometimes in dreams, but very ancient
faces, some in profile with hooked noses, some with
gentle smiles and closed eyes. Tracing out these faces
fascinated me so much that I was silent for a long time.

The fire was a continuing source of wonder. Gazing
into its shifting and hissing depths, I saw an extraordinary sight. There was a branch with buds of apple blos-
som upon it, probably culled from one of Angharad's
old trees. As I watched, the warmth caused the buds
to open. For a moment I gazed at the perfect flowers,
until the flames caught them too and quickly reduced
the whole branch to ashes. I felt that Trewyn and I
were like the buds coming into flower in our youth and
beauty, one day achieving our moment of perfection,
then returning to the nothingness from which we came.

"Are you still frightened?" I asked her.

"Oh, no, not at all. Well, not of being a *doran*. It's
what we have to be, isn't it? You and me. It's what
we're meant for, don't you think?"

WARM FROM THE HEAT of the fire, busy in the caverns
and passages of our own minds, Trewyn and I dozed,
propped up against the wooden chest. When I at last
awoke, Angharad and Euny were sitting once more on
the far side of the fire, looking as if they had never
disappeared. They sat still and silent, without a glance
in our direction.

They were different, however, as everything else was

different. Both of them had the same golden glow that I had noticed in the stones. The folds of the yellow shawl that Angharad wore seemed deep with mystery. Even Euny's worn black garments had a luminous sheen to them. Angharad's face, always full of kindness, now seemed so pure, generous, and good that I felt full of reverence as I looked at it. Euny's dark stern face held the desperate sadness of a lost little girl, yet I could see how gradually, painfully, that loneliness had grown into a great strength. Euny, I saw (though I felt I had always known this about her), was totally without fear. Whatever this strange uncomfortable ceremony was about, I decided that Angharad and Euny were to be trusted.

Euny was now building up the fire, though it was already hot in the hut, and Angharad had begun to chant a slow rhythmic melody. Trewyn and I had been taught the words and automatically joined in. As the heat grew in the hut, I could feel perspiration running down my face. Trewyn too looked desperately hot and turned anguished eyes to me. Yet Euny was still pushing twigs and logs into the fire.

Angharad and Euny now rose to their feet, and with Angharad making the mouth music that is common in her country, they began a sort of dance. It was nothing like the kind of merry occasion in which young men and women dance together. Rather it was as if Euny and Angharad were tracing out a pattern on the floor, seeking some knowledge with their feet. Occasionally they touched hands, turned toward or away from each other, led by the strange crooning cry of Angharad's singing, weaving the shape of the dance. First Trewyn, then I, got up and found ourselves irresistibly dancing with them with sure steps that no one had ever taught us. We danced, it seemed to me, for hours, weaving and dipping, turning and touching hands. Sometimes we danced—sometimes the dance danced us.

I think after this we all slept in total exhaustion. I was aware of waking once, cold since the fire had died down, stiff from the iron hardness of the ground, and desperately hungry. I could see daylight under the door, and I longed briefly to be part of that world outside, but sleep mercifully drew me back again into its embrace.

MUCH LATER, Trewyn was shaking me.

"Wake up! Look, the door's open!"

With an enormous effort I threw off the web of sleep. I could smell sweet fresh air through the open door—though both Trewyn and I were shivering with cold. We could see the dark sky with a few stars twinkling in it. There was no sign of Angharad or Euny.

"What do we do now?" I asked.

Without further conversation we left the hut with its dead embers. High up on the hill by the standing stones we caught sight of a bonfire and moved toward it. Cold and disheveled, wondering what fresh ordeals awaited us, we stumbled into the ring of standing stones and then stopped in astonishment. Angharad and Euny stood by the fire, as if waiting. Angharad wore a shining brown cloak clasped with yellow stones, and Euny wore a cloak figured in green and yellow and black. They signaled us to join them by the fire. Each had a bundle at her feet, and I was surprised to recognize the cloak I had so laboriously woven lying on the ground beside Euny. She came to me with a soft white tunic which she lifted over my head so that the folds fell to my feet. She fastened it at the neck, tied a girdle around my waist, then took a comb made of bone and combed the earth and tangles from my hair. She placed a pair of deerskin slippers on my feet, then lifted the heavy cloak and, easing it over my shoulders, joined the topaz clasp. It was lovely to feel the cloak's warmth and weight.

Meanwhile Angharad had also dressed Trewyn. When all was done, they embraced both of us, and Trewyn, in her warm, affectionate way, turned and hugged me. I could see in her eyes the thought that now we were really sisters.

Angharad took a loaf of wheaten bread and broke it in her strong fingers. She handed each of us a piece, and I ate mine eagerly. Even in my hungriest days with Euny food had never tasted as good as this. I could smell the wheat and the yeast in it, taste the salt. Then Angharad passed us a big cup of wine, and we each took a long drink. There was a spicy taste to it, and I guessed that she had added some secret herb. Just then, white and ghostlike in the starlight, I saw great wings floating above me, and there, big and silent, was Moon.

15

ACK IN Angharad's house the next morning, Trewyn and I made an odd discovery. "Watch this," she said to me. "I've just discovered it."

There was a moment's pause and then her smock, which was lying over a chair, got up—that is the only word for it—moved across the room, and flopped down on the floor. There was another pause, during which I could feel her concentrating hard, and then her smock rose up again and returned to the place it had come from.

I was impressed and at once determined to outdo her. A candle stood on the table, the one that had lighted us to bed the night before. I closed my eyes and concentrated, thinking only of the candle. When I opened them again, the candle was alight! Trewyn then extinguished the candle without moving from her bed, I lit it again, and she put it out.

"I know," said Trewyn, "let's see if we can make something. Both of us together." We agreed on a spider and almost at once a spider ran across the floor.

In the days that followed, both of us had a passion for trying out our new skills. We hid this from Angharad and Euny, sensing that they would think us very frivolous, but we simply could not stop. As soon as we were alone together or out for a walk, we would start on our trumpery magic. It was the greatest fun and we found it difficult to believe that we would ever tire of it. I am sure that Angharad at least, hearing the shouts of laughter that came from our room, knew very well what we were up to, but she never said a word. Perhaps she reflected that our time together was coming to an end.

We had changed in another way too since the day of the ceremony.

"Do you notice something different about your sense of smell?" I asked Trewyn tentatively one day. She nodded.

"I can smell you and Angharad and Euny—not just the usual human smells, but *something else*. It's as if they tell me something, just as the expression on a person's face tells you something about them. I can smell Angharad's goodness and Euny's strength. I can smell your healing wisdom."

"And I can smell your beauty!"

We asked Angharad about it and she confirmed, as if surprised that we would even ask, that smell was one of the skills of a *doran*.

IT WAS EARLY SUMMER when Euny and I set off for home, and our journey this time was pleasant. The hedgerows were fragrant with roses and honeysuckle, the meadowsweet billowed beneath them, the sky was a wide, cloudless blue, and we heard the cuckoo sing its late song. As we crossed the meadows, skylarks high above us rinsed our ears with their joyful din. We walked along the edges of cornfields full of young grain, past gardens from which we helped ourselves to tender pea pods, through misty blue woods, through dim forests, and over gentle hills. Sometimes, far away, we could see the glimmer of the sea. This time we slept warmly at night, full of Angharad's oatcake and fermented whey. One evening, as we ate our supper, Euny surprised me.

"Angharad said I did not feed you properly. Because I eat little I forget that young things need their food. I'll try to do better."

Euny said this without embarrassment or shame, but just as a fact. Angharad had pointed it out to her, and now she understood. I was touched.

"It's all right," I said awkwardly.

I had felt very sad at leaving Trewyn and Angharad, not to mention the comfort of Angharad's house, but I found that I took pleasure in being alone again with Euny, that although no word of affection was expressed and there were no embraces, her austere warmth toward me gladdened and pleased me. Since the time in the stone hut she seemed a little more friendly, as if she was sure of me in some way. The long days in the open air and nights of sound sleep made me feel extraordinarily well.

AS WE CAME OUT of the forest near Euny's hut and I saw the great shadow of the tor above us, I felt a little shiver of excitement and joy. It was not dark, but already a brilliant sliver of moon hung in the sky over the tor. Rain had made a pool on the grass in front of the hill and sitting upon it were twelve swans, their beautiful heads and wings mirrored in the water. The sun shone upon the tor at an angle that lit it strangely. Its bare, terraced sides were shadowed, its outline haloed. Euny and I stood quite still and Euny made some exclamation under her breath—it might have been an incantation or a prayer.

After a few moments she walked on, and I followed. The hut, with its dead embers, some moldering pig hanging on a hook from the ceiling, threadbare rug, and pathetic bits of furniture seemed unwelcoming, dusty, and cold, and for a moment my heart sank. Bearing the rotting carcass outside under Euny's orders, however, I saw the moon through the branches of the hazel tree and the outline of the hill springing behind it, and I knew that this was the place where I should be.

Euny had seated herself with unusual weariness in her old rocking chair. I lit a fire, swept and dusted, and made soup with the remains of the vegetables that Angharad had given us. Going outside to gather herbs, I saw the empty pigsty and remembered the incident before we had left home.

After supper I counted on my fingers. "Three months before I go back to my parents," I said. Euny nodded.

"There is a lot to do," she said. As always with Euny,

I could not bring myself to ask *what* there was to do, and she never explained.

WITHIN A FEW DAYS Euny and I had fallen straight back into our old routines. There were the household chores, the long silences, the meager meals. But Angharad's words had driven her to try harder to feed me. On the day after we returned home she disappeared without a word and came back several hours later laden with a large sack of wheaten flour. I immediately started making bread and cakes with it, as Angharad had taught me. On other days she returned with eggs and honey and cabbages and a set of newly hatched chicks, which she gave to me to rear. I was enchanted by their furry little bodies and loved to pick them up in my hands. When some of them died, as chicks do, I grieved over them, to Euny's irritation.

It seems to me now that I needed someone, something, to love. I missed Angharad and Trewyn badly. Though Euny noticed every flower and berry and cloud and turn of the wind, it felt as if she could live with *me* only by forgetting and ignoring me for much of the time.

Angharad had given me some material to make a pallet for myself, and after I stuffed the bag with straw I was able to sleep much more comfortably and warmly at night. She had also made me a blanket, in a brilliant pattern of dusky orange and midnight blue. I was never cold beneath it and it hung over the back of the rocking chair by day, giving the room a vivid focus. I picked flowers too, taking one of our few bowls to set them in.

I was out in the meadow near the hut one day picking some wild lilies when I heard the sound of hoofs on the trail. And there was my beloved Gamal! I was so thrilled to see him that it took me a few moments to notice that there was another rider behind him. To my dismay it was Finbar. Gamal gave a whoop of pleasure at seeing me, shouted to Finbar, and came across the field. Then Gamal and I began to talk. He wanted to know where I had been—he had come several times in search of me. I wanted to hear about everyone at Castle Dore. He had brought me a present from Meroot—some wind-dried meat that was a special delicacy among our people. Finbar listened patiently, smiling. Since their last visit, I had considered Finbar a sort of enemy, but he seemed perfectly friendly toward me. It was disconcerting.

"We thought we could stay here overnight and then spend tomorrow together," said Gamal. My heart sank slightly. How would I persuade Euny to let me have the day to myself?

"I'll go and ask Euny," I said nervously.

Euny was sitting and rocking herself placidly in the hut, and in the way that was typical of her she knew what I had come to ask before I asked it.

"They needn't think I'm going to feed them," she said.

"Couldn't we?" I pleaded. "We've plenty of meal."

Euny did not answer.

"I could make some porridge or something . . ."

"And you can't have the time off to play with them. We have a lot of work to do."

I felt furious both at her lack of hospitality and her

unfairness. I went out, slamming the hut door behind
me.

Gamal noticed my crestfallen expression at once.

"It's all right," he said. "We can sleep out in the
meadow in our blankets."

"She won't give you any food," I said. I had grown
up in a tradition that treated the guest as sacred, and I
felt humiliated.

"We've got enough in our saddlebags."

"But I *will* come out with you tomorrow. I'll pretend
to be going to the well to get water and then I'll run
off with you."

Finbar, I could see, admired me for this, but Gamal
looked a bit worried.

"Won't you get into awful trouble?" he asked.

I shrugged. The thought of a day's fun was worth it.

The next morning I set off with my buckets, left them
lying by the well, and ran off with Gamal and Finbar.
We rode to a distant beach, splashed in the sea for
hours, climbed rocks, and sunned ourselves. Gamal
played to us on his flute. Then I rode Gamal's pony
along the sand. It was wonderful to feel the motion of
a horse beneath me.

"You do ride well," Finbar said admiringly, and my
heart slightly softened toward him, though I gave no
indication of this. Also, when he caught a fish he came
and presented it to me as if giving me a present. But I
scarcely acknowledged it. I could not forget the shame
of the occasion when I had killed the pig, and the
mockery in Finbar's eyes at a moment when I was so
unhappy. In any case, I wanted Gamal to myself. As if

sensing my wish to be alone with Gamal, Finbar went off for a long ride by himself.

"How's Meroot?" I asked Gamal. A shadow crossed his face and he shrugged without replying. What he wanted to talk about was music. A new musician had come to court since I had left and was secretly teaching Gamal.

"It's not so much playing that interests me now. I have started to make up music. One night at dinner Evert sang a song I had composed and Meroot said how beautiful it was—without knowing it was mine, of course."

"She would never let you be a musician, would she?"

"No one can stop me from thinking of music—not even Meroot," said Gamal.

As the afternoon wore on, I grew a bit fearful of going back to confront Euny.

"Do you want us to come with you?" Gamal asked.

"No, go on home," I said. Gamal promised to come again, but I felt very sad as they cantered off along the beach.

I noticed as I passed the well that the buckets were still lying there, so I filled them and took them back with me. Euny was sitting in the rocking chair as if she had spent the whole day there. I braced myself for a scolding, but none came. In fact, I had an odd sort of feeling that she was rather pleased with me. I could not understand it at all. In fact, it was quite disturbing.

THREE

16

THE NEXT DAY Euny suddenly started to instruct me in the way I had longed for at the beginning, sitting me down and giving me long hours of teaching about spells, herbs, good magic, and bad magic. First she made me give demonstrations of the sort of skills Trewyn and I had practiced—making things move, appear, and disappear—then told me sternly that that was quite enough and that she hoped I would never waste my energies with that kind of thing again.

"Different *doran*s have different gifts," she said. "Yours will be to do with healing people, which is partly about a special kind of knowing and partly about a long and difficult study of herbs."

I was surprised that Euny took my healing gifts seriously.

"Oh, I knew about the healing because of the white owl," she said. "It was perfectly obvious. All those under the protection of the owl know about healing."

"What is the special kind of knowing?" I asked her.

"Being able to pay attention to people. Not just with your mind but with every part of you. Then you see the sickness quite clearly. I cannot help you with that. What I can teach you before you go home is the lore of herbs. As well as some other healing skills."

Euny had, of course, taught me to recognize many herbs in my first weeks with her. Now the task was to learn their uses by heart, to discover how to combine them, how to make them into pills and ointments, decoctions, tinctures, and teas. She had me reciting endlessly.

"Elecampane root, powdered, for coughs, and for those who cannot breathe . . . tincture of dwarf elder for dropsy . . . horsebane for piles. Dock for a purgative. Comfrey root boiled for inward hurts and for the spitting of blood . . . fresh comfrey root upon fresh wounds, cuts, and broken bones. Dried coltsfoot leaves and roots to be burned and the smoke drawn into the mouth through a reed with wine for a persistent cough. Culverwort to be used for sore throats. Yellow bugle, if you can obtain it, to cleanse the urine. Bistort to cure worms in children, catnip for colds . . ." It went on and on, hour after hour.

She taught me to make clearwater, the colorless liquid that protects a *doran* against sorcery, steeping rowan leaves with herbs in water where gold has lain. She explained to me about the terrible curses used by sorcerers which bring slow and miserable death to those who are their victims, and then recounted some of the rituals great *doran*s have used to dissolve the curses.

"There is no one way of doing it—you just have to use your wits and your imagination—but remember that earth, air, fire, and water are your allies . . ."

She taught me what to do for someone who has had a "sad" spell laid on them by a sorcerer, or the kind of spell that makes all places and people strike deadly fear. Even more important, she said, was to know what to do for a person who was "ghosted"—that is, captured and enslaved by a sorcerer in such a way that they no longer had a will or mind of their own. She told me of sorcerers who gave drinks to their enemies that made them appear like dead people. Their relatives buried them in great sadness. Then the "corpse" woke up in the coffin, was dug up and spirited away by the sorcerer, and forced to work as a slave in a distant place. Of course, nobody wondered what had happened to them. Suddenly I remembered Gamal's description of the dreadful picture in Meroot's parchments.

The spells and recipes Euny taught me were long and complicated, but all of them were to bring about good or prevent evil. The only way to be sure of them was to learn them by heart and then to repeat them to her time after time, which she made me do endlessly, until she was quite sure I had mastered them. She would not permit me to change even unimportant words, but insisted that I repeat the words she used, even, it seemed to me, in her exact tone of voice. I was so interested in what she was teaching me that I found this laborious learning quite pleasurable.

Now the weeks passed very quickly. Once or twice Gamal came again, this time alone.

"Tell me truly about Meroot," I said, remembering his reluctance to speak of her. "Is something wrong with her? Is she ill?"

"Not as you mean it. Only I think there *is* something wrong with her."

"Can you explain?"

"I will tell you what I think. It is that she still dreams that one day, when your father is dead, I will take over his kingdom."

Embarrassed, Gamal looked away from me out over the countryside.

"Would you want to do that?" I asked, my voice wobbling at the thought of my father dead.

"That is not the point. Last birthday I swore my allegiance to the king. Plotting against him is against the rule of the knights."

I was silent, not knowing what to say.

"There is something else." Gamal's voice cracked with shame and anguish. "You know that Meroot can do magic, is . . . perhaps . . . a sorcerer. I'm afraid of what she might do."

I shivered with fear of Meroot but put out a hand and patted Gamal's hand.

"I will be back home soon," I said. "Then we can talk more of these things. Perhaps I could warn my father." Gamal shook his head gloomily, as if in doubt that we could save the situation.

That night I told Euny about the conversation, and she listened with her head on one side like a bird.

"Your magic is at least as strong as Meroot's magic,"

she said. "You have been well taught. There is perhaps only one other who may be stronger."

"Who is the other?"

"A sorcerer in Caerleon."

"Angharad's old enemy!"

I shivered at the dangers hidden in her words. "I must try to oppose Meroot, then?"

Euny spoke dryly. "Perhaps it was for this that you were born."

The relationship between Euny and me had suddenly become quite different. Instead of treating me as her servant, Euny now did her full share of the household chores—fetching water from the well, cleaning out the fire, preparing meals, sweeping and tidying. There was a note of respect, of listening to what I said, which I did not remember from before. For the first time since I had come to live with her there was a sense of peace, of pleasantness and ease, which reminded me of the life of Angharad and Trewyn.

As day by day Euny imparted her secrets to me, I knew that the seasons were wheeling to the place when I must soon again return to my parents, though I knew too that at some time in the future I would come back to Euny for the rituals that would complete my training as a *doran*.

"What will happen when I go back home?" I asked Euny. "Must I marry?"

"Do you want to marry?" she asked.

"I don't know. Not yet, anyway. I'm only a child."

"Who will rule the kingdom when your father dies?" Euny asked sharply. "Will it be you?"

I shrugged. "Because women are not warriors, it is difficult for them to rule."

"I don't see why," said Euny. "There are other important things in kingship besides warfare."

"I'm not sure if I could rule," I said uncertainly. "What difference will being a *doran* make? I thought it was a vocation of its own."

"You will have to see," said Euny unhelpfully.

"Will you miss me when I am gone?" I rashly asked her.

Euny tossed her head in a gesture I knew well.

"I need nobody," she said. "Certainly not you."

I was not as crushed as I would formerly have been.

"Well, I will miss you," I said, "and I believe that you will miss me." I could see by the obstinate gleam in her eye that she had no intention of giving me the satisfaction of telling me she cared for me.

On the day of my departure for Castle Dore, Euny watched me as I lowered Moon gently from his perch and put him into his traveling bag.

"I am coming with you to help you carry your things," Euny said suddenly. Since I had nothing but my *doran*'s cloak, and Angharad's blanket, and a little food and water for the journey, that was scarcely necessary, and I knew she was merely using it as an excuse.

"I will miss the hut," I said, looking around it for the last time.

"It will still be here," said Euny pettishly. "You can come and see it when you can spare the time from your grand life."

I wept a little as we walked through the forest. I felt as if nothing would console me for the loss of those hard days which now, I realized, had taught me a great deal. I would not see the tor, nor the hazel tree, when I woke up each morning. I would not see Euny.

When Castle Dore appeared in the distance Euny stopped. She put her hands into the folds of her gown and brought out two large flasks and some other objects and laid them on the ground in front of her.

"Here are your 'protections,'" she told me, using the *doran* word. "If there is the slightest chance of your running into danger, you must carry them with you at all times."

One of the protections was a crescent moon on a leather string, and Euny put it over my head with the air of investing me with an honor. The next thing she gave me was a black egg.

"If you are in danger of your life you may break this egg," she said. "But be careful. If you do it when the danger is not severe, you will be unprotected when the real danger comes. As come it will, early or late. So use it wisely."

"But how will I *know?*" I said in a sort of wail, already certain that I would break the egg at the wrong moment. Euny gave me a withering look and did not deign to answer.

"Clearwater you know about," she added, giving me the two flasks. "After this you must make your own."

I tucked away all the protections into my bundle and then looked up to speak to Euny, but she was gone!

The long straight path was quite empty, only it seemed to me that I could hear her cackle of laughter echoing in the air.

I walked on soberly. I was nervous about my return. As I approached Castle Dore, I was surprised to see a great flock of rooks wheeling about the place. I had never seen rooks there before, and their black wings and persistent cries gave an air of menace.

The guards saluted when I reached the entrance—I found my way quickly through the trick of the maze and into the big enclosure of the castle. The doors of the hall and the council chamber stood open wide, so I knew my father must be elsewhere. I went straight to my parents' quarters and found my mother reading and my father writing on his tablet. The glimpse I caught of him through the lattice before he saw me suggested that he was worried—he looked older, bent with care.

I stood in the doorway.

"I have come back."

My mother and father embraced me and made me feel that I was glad to be back at the Wooden Palace after all.

"Tell me," said the king, "did Euny teach you all that you hoped?"

"It was very hard," I told him. "But I learned more, much more than I knew there was to learn."

"And you have come back here to marry?"

"I don't know," I said. "Do you wish me to marry?"

My father hesitated, exchanging glances with my mother as if weighing up different ideas in his mind, then said, "We will talk of this later. Tonight we will have a feast for your return. See that you wear a fine gown—not that rag you have on your back—and that your hair is dressed with jewels."

I bowed before him because, after all, he was the king, and I went to my old apartment.

It was strange to be back in the comforts of Castle Dore. Although my own chamber was cold and empty, Erith soon bustled in, embraced me with joy, and lit a fire. While I waited, she had a servant bring me a plate of chicken and some white bread, which I ate hungrily. She summoned other servants, who brought water heated in the kitchen. As she had done so often in the past, she bathed me—exclaiming in horror at the calluses on my hands and the blisters on my feet and observing how thin I was—then she dressed me in a yellow silk gown that went well with my dark hair. She found a fillet of silver and bound my hair with it, then placed a torque of silver around my neck and bracelets on my arms. When I looked at myself in the big bronze mirror, I saw how grown-up I had become—very different from the child who had last sought her reflection there. I was slender and pretty, I thought with youthful pride, and the heat of the fire had brought a pleasing pink to my cheeks. When I went to join my father I held my head high. King Mark's daughter had come home.

My father was expecting me and gave me a long appreciative look and a smile. He was obviously pleased. Together we walked to the Great Hall, where his knights waited to dine with him, and together we walked through the big room while the pipes and drums played for us. I sat beside his carved chair in my smaller one, and when he took up his knife he cut a piece of roast swan and presented it to me—the custom used by my people to make a guest welcome.

The evening proceeded as I remembered many evenings doing in the past—the slow meal that I had always found so tedious once my appetite was satisfied. There were a number of courses, but—was it my imagination?—there seemed to be less food than there had been in the past. While we ate, a bard sang a song of love and adventure.

Perhaps because I had lived such a simple life with Euny, because I was genuinely hungry, or because my recent experiences had made me look at the world with a fresh eye, everything tonight seemed wonderfully interesting. I enjoyed the faces of the knights—some of them old and scarred with battle, others still in the pride of young manhood. I savored the bright colors of the clothes and jewels, the harmonies of the music, the glorious taste and smell of the food, the rich scent and ruby tint of the wine, the beauty and intelligence of the dogs that crouched beside my father. I laid my hand upon my father's.

"It is good to be back," I told him.

Afterward, as we sat near the fire, the knights came up and talked to me—men who had known me as a child. The young squires, no older than I was myself, who had sat at the lowest table, eyed me shyly, one or two of them looking as if they would like to talk. I went about the room, enjoying the lively company and the handsome young men. Yet . . . many of them had a pallor, a kind of weariness about them that puzzled me. Surely they had not always been like that?

Even after my father had left the hall I stayed, talking and laughing. At one moment my eyes strayed toward the door. Two tall boys were leaving and one of them was half turned, laughing, to catch a comment the other had made. It was Gamal and Finbar. Gamal waved and Finbar bowed with just the faintest suggestion of friendly mockery. I grinned back at them.

Later, in my parents' quarters, I sat on a footstool between them, as I had often done as a child. In reply to their questions I told them a little more of my life with Euny and asked them about life at Castle Dore.

But I could see a shadow cross my mother's face, and my father moved like an old man in his chair. He was very thin, I noticed.

"There is trouble?" I asked him, expecting a story of raids and plundering, of the need to lead his young men to some horrific battle from which many would not return. He clasped and unclasped his hands in a wretchedness I had not seen before. He was not a fearful man, and had always had a certain appetite for the excitement of war, though he grieved at the human cost.

A look of shame and pain crossed his face.

"The crops have done badly," said my mother. "Many animals have died for no reason that we can discover."

"Is it magic?" I asked.

"There have always been years when the crops failed," said my father crossly, "and years when the animals have been sick."

"Not often both together," said my mother pointedly.

"Do you suspect anyone?" I asked her. She did not answer, but again exchanged a glance with my father, and I guessed that they had had many conversations on this subject.

"We cannot speak of it tonight," she said. "It is late. Come and see us tomorrow and I will say more."

17

THE NEXT MORNING there was a light tap on my door at dawn. Accustomed to early rising, I was already awake. I opened the door quietly, so I would not disturb Erith, and found Gamal waiting outside.

"Come out for a ride!" he whispered. In a few moments I was dressed. He had two horses saddled and ready, and soon we were miles away on a hillside overlooking the sea. We breakfasted out of the wind in a hollow—Gamal had thoughtfully brought bread and some cold meat.

"Is it good to be back?" he asked me.

I hesitated.

"It is lovely to be home, but . . . my father seems ill, and he tells me that the harvest was so bad he fears famine."

Gamal nodded. He looked miserable, I thought.

"Something is very wrong," I added. He was silent,

but I felt that there was more he could have said if he had chosen to. Then he mentioned a piece of court news that I had already heard: Meroot intended to marry again.

"A knight from Caerleon," he said. The name stirred some troubling memory in me, though I could not think what it was.

"She will marry in December," said Gamal shortly. "The king is to give a great feast for her."

AS WE RETURNED HOME, I noticed a sort of bleakness about the countryside that I did not remember from previous autumns. The sheep looked sickly and listless, the people gray and afraid. Even at Castle Dore, now that I was no longer excited to be back, I saw that everyone looked pale, tired, and dispirited.

The next day I called upon Meroot, as etiquette dictated, to greet her upon my return and to congratulate her upon her marriage. She received me in the little house my father had built for her—she had never ceased complaining about its smallness—and we drank a sweet tawny wine from across the sea and ate honey biscuits. The room was very bare, save for an odd-looking leather stick that stood propped against the wall.

Meroot wore a gray gown with a turquoise and silver collar; her wrists were heavy with jewelry of jet and silver. She was accompanied by a huge black hound that I had never seen before, collared, like her, in turquoise and silver. The hound was so big I could not take my eyes off it. A pastille burned in a dish, giving the room a scent of lilies, yet somewhere beneath that scent there were other smells, sharp and sour and sickening.

"So what did Euny teach you?" Meroot wished to know. Though it was the same question my father had asked, the way it was asked was quite different.

"She taught me healing arts," I said carefully. "She taught me the doses for sicknesses and the way of touching to make people well. And Angharad of the West taught me to spin and weave."

"Angharad!" she said in obvious surprise.

"Do you know her?"

"I did once."

The silence fell heavily between us, until Meroot left the room to fetch more wine. She closed the door behind her and I glanced around. The leather stick caught my eye again and I stood up and moved toward it. Immediately the black hound growled softly in its throat and moved between me and the stick. I sat down uneasily. Suddenly I had the oddest feeling that I was being watched, that through a knot in the door or a hole in the tapestry Meroot's cold blue eye was fixed upon me. I composed myself as unselfconsciously as possible and wondered why she would do such a thing. What could she see that she could not observe when she sat in front of me?

At that moment the outer door opened and Gamal came in, hot and weary, wearing parts of his armor and carrying the rest over his arm. He smiled and started telling me of his latest lesson, then sat down, filthy as he was from the practice field. It seemed to me that once again I heard the dog growl softly in its throat, though it did not move. But then Meroot came back, the dog slunk into a corner, and Gamal and I fell silent. I was glad when I could go home without appearing rude.

My mother was alone that afternoon when I called upon my parents.

"It's Meroot, isn't it?" I said without delay. "You are afraid she is laying a curse upon Castle Dore."

Erlain nodded.

"Your father won't hear of it. He is loyal to her, and it is destroying the kingdom." Erlain's eyes filled with tears. "I was wondering, Ninnoc. Do you know any magic that might help us?"

My first thought was to send for Euny, but then I remembered that she had gone away on a visit to Angharad. I felt both excited and frightened. I had not dreamed that I might need to use my new skills so soon. "Let me think about it," I said. Before I left Erlain, I gave her a flask of Euny's clearwater and told her how to anoint herself with it.

"See if you can persuade Father to use it too," I said, not very hopefully. Lying in bed, I thought about the careful schooling I had had in magic—how I had learned all that my wise teacher could tell me. Now I would find out if my education was equal to the challenge. Just as I was falling asleep I remembered, with a start that woke me right up again, that it was at Caerleon that Trewyn had encountered a sorcerer and been saved by Angharad. Who was the sinister enemy of Angharad Trewyn had once described to me? Suppose, just suppose, it was Meroot's new husband. Was this why

Meroot was startled to hear Angharad's name? If she had not known it before, Meroot now knew that Angharad and Euny were friends.

ALREADY THE PLANS were going forward for Meroot's wedding. Wines were being taken from our cellars; pigs, chickens, and swans were being fattened; deer were being hunted. Soon we would start making pies, baking, and roasting.

Gifts for the bride from the Gray Knight of Caerleon began to arrive: silks and spices, scents and rare fruits, inlaid boxes containing jewels, nightingales in cages, fine hunting hawks, beautiful ponies with snowy coats and bright enameled harnesses. The knight's presents were so many and frequent that they became the object of jokes around the Wooden Palace—there was not much to joke about just then—but it was evident that the knight either loved Meroot or needed her good will. It was clear too that he was a rich man.

I can still remember the set look on Gamal's face as the knight's servants arrived day after day bearing gifts.

"You know, they wish me to go with them to live at Caerleon," he said.

"You won't go?"

"I don't want to . . ." I knew of Gamal's loyalty to his mother, a loyalty I had only once seen waver.

THE PREPARATIONS at Castle Dore speeded up—the bards composed new songs and the smell of roasting meat pervaded everything. The kingdom was short of food, yet the rules of hospitality demanded that guests should be richly entertained. On the night before the Gray Knight's arrival, my father gave a feast for Meroot in the Great Hall and she sat beside him in the seat where my mother or I usually sat. Her pale face was flushed, her eyes sparkled, and there was an odd sort of triumph about her that troubled me. Sitting directly opposite her, I could not avoid her gaze, nor the need to make conversation.

"You will live at the house of the Gray Knight?" I asked her. She described it to me and it sounded very splendid. Yet gazing into her strange light eyes, so lacking in depth or feeling, I felt as I had felt as a small child: her apparent amiability concealed an intense hatred of me. I remembered my father telling me of Meroot's longing, as a little girl, to outstrip him at everything— at running, at shooting with a bow, at climbing trees, or at the civilized arts of singing and oration. For the first time I felt sympathy for Meroot—it was hard to be a girl in a royal family and see your younger brother preferred to you for no better reason than that he was a boy. I, who had no brothers, was far luckier than she—I am sure she thought this. All the same, because I was a girl I was vulnerable to Meroot's scheming.

I slept fitfully, tossing and turning, and woke just before the cold, gray dawn. I got up quietly and went out, as I had done so often when I was restless or anxious, to walk around the ramparts and the big ditch beyond them. I hailed the sleepy sentries and began a slow pacing. It was bitter cold, and I drew my cloak warmly around me, but I enjoyed watching the light gradually ascending over the valleys. Then, with a sense of shock, I saw the figure of a woman in a field outside, her face turned to the Wooden Palace. I realized it was Meroot. She could not see me—I was no more than a small face above the parapet and it was still fairly dark— and she went on with what she was doing, moving widdershins, holding up her hand and making signs in the direction of the palace, occasionally dipping her fingers into a bowl she held in her other hand. As the dawn gradually replaced the dark, I saw that her upraised hand was stained a dull red; the bowl must contain blood. I could not hear her voice or see her mouth move, but I had no doubt at all that she was uttering spells.

18

THAT DAY the Gray Knight arrived, celebrated by a trumpeter as he entered our gates and surrounded by pages who carried more presents for Meroot, including a magnificent collar of pearls. He was received by my father, and they spent half the day talking together. I met the knight when the evening brought us all together in the Great Hall.

He was a tall, handsome man, carrying, as many of the knights did, scars of battle on his face. In his case, they only added to his good looks. He had piercing black eyes, and when he was introduced to me, I felt as if he looked right through me and knew everything about me. For the first time since my return I felt afraid. The sight of Gamal's miserable face as he stood beside Meroot did not reassure me.

The wedding was celebrated with great splendor, and as was our custom, the feast went on for days. Like most of the younger people, I got bored with the end-

less drinking and storytelling and soon slipped away to
talk and have fun. Freed from Meroot's supervision,
Gamal and I spent a lot of time together. Quite often
we were joined by Finbar, who, despite myself, I was
beginning to like. Gamal often played his flute, pausing
from time to time to share the thoughts that troubled
him.

"They'll make me go back to Caerleon with them,"
he said. "The trouble is, I'm not old enough to refuse."

"One of the knights could make you his squire," Finbar suggested.

Gamal shook his head. Both of us knew the reason
this was unlikely: if Meroot wanted him to accompany
her, none of the knights would wish to defy her.

"Do you think now that Meroot is married she will
give up her plans for Castle Dore—you know, the ones
you told me about that time at the shore?"

This was not quite honest of me. The memory of
Meroot cursing us all in the winter dawn did not suggest that her ambitions had changed.

Gamal shook his head and flushed.

"She has never forgiven your father for inheriting
the kingdom and taking it from her. She believes it is
rightly hers—and eventually mine." He hesitated for a
long while. "She thinks only of how to get it back. She
will not forgive me for refusing to help her. I think
that is why she bore me and why she insists I must be
a soldier. So that somehow I can avenge her."

"What will she do to get what she believes is hers?
Will she fight for it, or will she prefer to use spells?" I
tried to keep my voice as even as possible, as if we

were discussing something that did not matter very much.

Gamal shrugged.

"I have no doubt she is using spells already. As to war . . . I do not know."

"For a moment, the other night, I felt sorry for Meroot," I said. "It is not fair that she was robbed of the throne. I would not like it if a younger brother was preferred before me—if I wanted to be queen, that is."

"But she swore loyalty to King Mark, as we all did. He has been good to us and . . . you are my cousin and friend."

I put out a hand and grasped Gamal's.

"In any case, curses are no way to get what you want." So Gamal really did think, as I did, that Meroot's curse was what ailed the country.

It was a great relief when Meroot and the Gray Knight rode back to Caerleon along with their retinue of servants. The knight's servants had been rude and arrogant, and the feast had strained the slender resources of Castle Dore. Though, of course, I watched Gamal ride away with a sad heart. My friend and ally had left us.

Yet almost immediately I was distracted by a new piece of information. Visiting my mother, I found her in a strange state, both elated and anxious.

"Ninnoc, it is unmistakable . . . I am to have a baby!"

I knew that she had longed to have another child, and that although she loved me, her only daughter, she had felt somehow to blame for not providing the warrior-heir that kings preferred. I also knew that if she did have a boy, it meant that I would never become queen. I felt a pang of jealousy. I tried to crush it beneath the protective feelings I had about my mother.

"Don't tell anyone for as long as possible in case Meroot finds out," I cautioned.

"That is why I am afraid," said Erlain, her great gray eyes filled with dread. "That she may know already and have damaged my child."

"You used the clearwater?"

"Yes. Every day."

"It will be all right. This comes at a good time. It will comfort people that something—someone—can live and grow despite Meroot's curse."

I had been giving a lot of thought to Meroot's curse, and as a result, I was sleeping badly. My nightmares were about Meroot, clad all in gray, and, more terrible, of a huge unblinking eye watching me through a hole in a wall. If only Euny were at home, I kept thinking, to give me advice. How could I undo the curse and turn Meroot's corrupting, killing hate into the love that made all things grow?

I turned over in my mind all that I had been taught. "Earth, air, fire, and water are your allies," Euny had said.

I planned the ritual and asked my mother to accompany me. The next morning I woke with a sense of fear—I felt as if I were directly challenging Meroot—but I got up, put on Euny's crescent moon necklace and my *doran*'s cloak, and lowered Moon onto my shoulder. Erlain and I went out before dawn to the place beyond the walls where I had seen Meroot. I stood still and thought of the mother goddess before whom Euny had bowed in her shrine high on the tor.

Then I took earth and crumbled it between my fingers.

"Mother, let sun and rain make this earth fertile. Let it yield crops to feed our animals and provide food for our children. Let the plants flower and the trees bear fruit. And let no human blood be spilled upon this earth."

I took water and poured it out on the ground.

"Mother," I said, "let our springs and streams and rivers run pure so that all may drink. Let this water wash away the curse of violence."

I lit a small fire.

"Mother, let this fire burn away all that is wicked and corrupt."

I stood and looked up into the dark sky.

"Mother, let the air of this place not be filled with cries of pain."

I turned to Erlain, the mother whom I knew and loved. Putting my hands gently on her belly, I thought of the baby within.

"Mother, keep this one safe," I asked. "May this child be born strong and healthy and grow up in a kingdom that knows peace."

Then, as Angharad and Euny had taught me, I danced the dance that is the harmony of all creation, and as I did so, I uttered the great words that keep sorrow and sickness within bounds. Finally I bowed low in the direction of the Wooden Palace.

When it was over, I felt desperately tired, almost too

weary to climb the path to Castle Dore. I had given
my strength to the anticurse, and it had left me feeling
weak and afraid. As we returned, I noticed with a sense
of pleasure and relief that the rooks were rising from
the trees on one side with noisy cries and flapping indignantly away.

WITHIN A FEW WEEKS it was plain that something was
very different in the kingdom. The ewes and cows and
horses began to conceive, and the people to regain their
old vitality. My mother had a new piece of information
for me.

"Ninnoc, I don't know what you will say. The astrologers tell me that the baby will be a boy!" Again I
felt that pang of jealousy and anger. It had not been
difficult to utter a *doran*'s blessing upon the new baby—
I could not possibly wish my mother any harm—yet I
knew that in my heart I had hoped the baby would be
a girl.

The winter months slipped away and the sun returned. That year we had a wonderful spring. The air
seemed full of the calling of birds, and the woods shone
with primroses, violets, and bluebells. Trees and
hedgerows were covered with blossoms, the sowing
produced strong green shoots, and the lambing was the
best we had ever had. After the fear and darkness of
the winter, people were lighthearted and joyous. They
were thin and short of food after their ordeals, but their
eyes were full of hope, and my father walked with a
light step. Meroot had gone, and her curse had gone
with her.

19

I HEARD NOTHING of Gamal for many weeks, and I missed him sorely. I worried that if Meroot's schemes were defeated, loyal Gamal might be made to suffer for it in some way. I could scarcely imagine that he was happy in the house of Meroot and the Gray Knight, knowing well that the best parts of his childhood had all been at moments when he was away from his mother.

Now that the immediate danger to Castle Dore had been averted, there seemed no real task for me there, nothing worthy of my energies or of my training as a *doran*. Euny, I reckoned, might be back by now from her visit to Angharad. I decided to go and see her, to tell her of what had passed since I left her and see whether she would give me any guidance about my future. Goodness knows she was obstinate enough in what she would and would not talk about, yet I was certain, somehow, that if my need was urgent enough, she would relent and tell me what I had to know.

I suppose I could have taken my pony and traveled faster, yet it seemed proper to approach Euny on foot, as I had done in the past. With little more than a change of clothing I made my way to her hut, navigating by the tor, passing through the forest without the fear I had once known. If she was not at home, I thought, I could spend a day or two at the hut and return, though I would be very disappointed not to see her. I was delighted, at the end of my long walk, to see smoke rising from her hut. Just as if she were awaiting me after an afternoon of herb gathering, she was sitting in her rocking chair, and one of her strange-smelling soups was bubbling on the fire.

I could tell from her smile that she was very glad to see me, though, as always, she did her best to hide her pleasure.

"Nothing better to do, I suppose," she said with a sniff.

"I was longing to see you, and I need your advice," I said.

"I know," she said. "I made the soup because you were coming."

"How did you know?" I asked, more for the pleasure of hearing what she would say than because I doubted her.

"I dreamed it," she said airily.

I had my familiar sense of being surprised by Euny— of always being on the wrong foot yet of rather enjoying it—and I laughed to myself as I sat down by the hearth. It seemed a long time since the day I had sat there with my swollen ankle and wept at the misery of becoming her apprentice.

Over supper I told her of the anticurse and how well it had worked. She listened attentively, her dark eyes watching me, and when I was done she gave a nod of approval.

"But I do not think Meroot has finished with us," I added. "I believe she means to take my father's kingdom by one means or another. There is the baby too. If my mother has a boy, then I shall not become queen." I tried to say this calmly, without feeling, but Euny was not deceived.

"You're jealous!" she said.

For a moment I hated her. Then I nodded.

"I am," I said.

Euny was silent for a long time. I had forgotten how slowly life moved around her.

"It is time to fly," she said at last. I knew that flying was an important adventure in the *doran* world—that it was a way of discovering where one's true vocation lay. I took a deep breath—the idea scared me—and said, "When?"

"The day after tomorrow. You will need to fast."

IN ORDER TO FLY you had to have a special brown ointment spread all over your skin. Then you sat very still and concentrated, usually with the help of your teacher, and if all went well you found yourself in another place. What you had to do there was to keep your eyes and ears open, and if you did it properly, then you often learned about the future, not so much ordinary details about what might happen to you—the sort that soothsayers provide—as a sense of the shape and meaning of it. It was easy to get frightened and will oneself back into ordinary life long before the end. I was determined that no matter what I saw, I would wait for the flying dream to leave me of its own accord rather than run away from it.

The day of fasting seemed very long, but as night-time came, Euny helped me bathe and then anointed me all over with the brown ointment, of which she kept a jar on a shelf. Then the two of us waited, standing face to face before the fire, our eyes fixed on each other. I felt a little sick, a little faint, but Euny willed me to stand upright while I waited for the moment of change. I would have given a lot to be somewhere else just then, but I tried to calm myself and wait. What changed everything was a sound like a tremendous cracking— the sort of sound a tree makes if it is snapped off in a winter gale—a noise so loud that I felt I lost conscious-ness for a moment. Then there was a strong pulling sensation, as if a hurricane were blowing me away and I was whirling through space so fast that it was hard to breathe. Not for long.

Almost at once, it seemed, I was in a dark place that reminded me of my old dream. I could hardly see, but I was running over sharp, slippery stones, and some-thing was coming after me, making a noise of splashing and snuffling. An appalling stench was in my nostrils, one I felt I ought to know but could not quite identify. Almost before the horror of this overtook me, the vi-sion changed. Now I could see clearly, and what I saw was Gamal's face, but it was upside down. At the same time I heard the sound of a child crying.

Then once again the pulling feeling had me in its power. I was being lifted, dragged, blown off the earth and had to submit again to being whirled in space. From high in the sky I looked down upon an island, and then I was standing on the island in front of a house. The house was white and stood upon a sort of inland cliff. I entered it, and there was a great hearth in the center of the room, the heart, I thought, of a place full of peace. Behind it were shelves with jars full of liquid, and when I looked out I could see a garden with neat rows of herbs. On the other side I could see that the land fell away, and in the distance was a view of a village and sea and shore. Feeling almost as if I were trespassing in someone's house and the owner might come home and catch me, I sat in a big chair by the hearth, watched thoughtfully by an owl—not Moon—who perched on a shelf. As I did so, my fears subsided. I knew that this was my chair and my house, that I fitted it perfectly and was completely comfortable, that this was the place in the world that I was seeking. It was a place in which there was no dread. From it I returned, after a while, to Euny's hut.

"I've found it," I reported with joy to Euny.

"What?"

"The place where I must be."

"Where is it?"

I described to her the house and the island, the inland cliff and the distant sea, and she nodded.

"I think I know where it is."

"Where?" I was breathless.

"If the flying dream wanted you to know that, it would

have told you," she said maddeningly. "In any case, that is far in the future. Was that all you saw?"

Much less happily I told her of the terror that had pursued me in the tunnel, of Gamal's face, and of the sound of crying. She looked grave.

"Do flying dreams make something happen to you, or are they what would have happened anyway?" I asked Euny.

"There is a part of you," said Euny, "that knows the future as well as it knows the past. It is not concerned with time. So that if you consult that part, which flying does, it can give you a memory of the future, just as your ordinary memory tells you about the past." She hesitated, her eyes fixed on mine as both of us struggled with this memory, a very fleeting and vague memory, in my case, of the future. I had a sense that something was being asked of me, some act of love or generosity that felt unbearably difficult.

"Something must be given up," I heard myself say to Euny, and she nodded encouragingly, as if that was just what she had seen herself, and she quoted under her breath a *doran* poem about "seeking with purity of spirit."

"How do you mean?" I asked, but she simply stared at me in reply, as if she had said quite enough.

"Gamal? How does he come into it? Why is he upside down?"

"Your love and friendship for him will be tested. Meroot, or perhaps the knight—they have power over Gamal at present." Euny looked past me now, as if painfully fixed on the future.

"And the terror in the tunnel?" I finally asked.

"You are a *doran*," said Euny. "A *good* one. I have seen to that. To be able to encounter evil, naked evil, that is your business. Not every day, not often, but when it is necessary. And now that you have found your place—through the flying—that makes it much easier. That is your center. It waits for you, and one day it will find you."

I RETURNED to Castle Dore scarcely knowing whether to feel pleased or sad. The joy and calm I had felt in my dream house with the great hearth taught me that one day I would truly find my place and my own peace in the world. How could anyone not rejoice at that? Yet somewhere in my life—presumably before I found my way to the island—lay the prospect of terror, with the unknown significance of the crying child. I didn't like that thought at all.

So not very cheerfully I set off on the long walk home. It felt comforting to see dear Castle Dore looking particularly beautiful as the evening sun shone upon its steep walls and low roofs.

"Your father wants you," Erith said as I was washing off the dust of my journey.

Something different about the king's face struck me as soon as I came into his chamber, and without asking anything about my visit to Euny he came straight to the point.

"I have heard from Meroot," he said. "Gamal is proposing marriage to you."

20

I WAS SO SURPRISED I sat down on a stool and stared at him dumbly.

"We're not old enough," I said at last. I knew very well, of course, that children my age, particularly royal children, did get married, but because Gamal was a friend I had always known, it had never occurred to me to think of him as a husband.

"In many ways it would be good," the king went on, ignoring my remark. "Meroot, I am sure, has minded that my birth robbed her of the throne. By this marriage of cousins she would feel gratified, and Castle Dore would have the protection of a warrior."

"As well as of a *doran*," I said crossly. At that moment I felt hurt and angry that my father so clearly preferred a boy as his successor. "But if Mother has a boy, Meroot won't get her wish anyway."

"That is true. We must consider both possibilities."

"Why don't we wait and see? There's no hurry, is there?"

I could see the king trying to decide how much to tell me, though the gravity of his expression told me much before he spoke.

"I am told," he said, "that the Gray Knight is pressing the countryside for soldiers. No one is quite sure"—his tone was very dry—"why he is recruiting them, but the rumor is that he means to attack Castle Dore."

I knew how painful this news must be to the king for several reasons, but I also saw how it affected my own position. The Gray Knight had let news of his activity reach us, but at the same time a marriage was suggested between Gamal and me. If I agreed, there would be no war. If I refused . . .

"You love Aunt Meroot, and you believe she loves you. Would she let the knight attack us?" I felt angry at my father's blindness about his sister. He did not reply, but a look of mingled shame and pain crossed his face.

"You *like* Gamal," he said. "He has been your dearest friend."

I thought of my dear friend with his honest eyes and his truthful tongue.

"I take it there is no word from Gamal himself," I said. There was not. Both of us fell silent, each thinking our thoughts. I was beginning to wonder why the flying dream had given me no hint of marriage, when the king startled me out of my reverie with his next words.

"Your aunt Meroot suggested that you visit

Caerleon, and I accepted the invitation on your behalf."

I reacted to this news with shock and disbelief.

"Father, these people wish to fight us! How can you send me to visit them?"

"There will be no danger to the kingdom if you marry Gamal. And I am certain that Meroot will take care of you." Nothing, I could see, would ever convince my father that Meroot was not to be trusted. All the same, I thought I would try once more.

"I don't trust Meroot. She is a dangerous woman. All she wants is to put Gamal on the throne. I don't want to go to Caerleon."

My father's face grew dark with rage. "You will do as I say."

I got up, inclined my head as etiquette demanded, and went out. Without hesitation I went in search of my mother.

"You know about the marriage suggestion? And that Meroot has invited me to Caerleon?"

She nodded. "I am sure the king knows it is wrong, but also that he fears to lose the kingdom to the Gray Knight."

"So I am to be the sacrifice?" I asked bitterly.

"We women are not asked whom we will marry. I was lucky that I loved your father. You could do worse than Gamal."

"And become the tool of Meroot and the Gray Knight?" My mother was silent.

In my anger I went out and paced around the Great Ditch. What I resented most was having no control over my life, of being a mere pawn, indeed a lost pawn, in the game being played between Meroot and my father. Suddenly an arrow whistled past my ear. I looked up, and there, fifty paces away, was Finbar grinning at me.

"That's dangerous," I said crossly. In my heart I had never quite forgiven Finbar.

"Let me come with you."

"What?"

"Let me come with you to Caerleon."

"How on earth do you know about that?" Castle Dore was always alive with gossip, but I knew my father had kept his moves fairly secret.

"I have been your father's messenger."

"Why do you want to go?"

"Because I am Gamal's friend and because . . ." With a slightly nervous gesture he looked up at the walls around us. He knew, as I did, that someone lying on the other side of the mound could hear every word that was said while remaining unseen. "Is there somewhere we could talk in private?"

We returned to my chamber and sat there together as Gamal and I had done so often in the past.

"I carried a message for your father to Caerleon. It is a grim place. Naturally, when my business was done, I asked to see Gamal. At first Meroot said that I could not see him. Then I told her that I had a message for him from you. And that you had said I must deliver it only to Gamal. She kept me waiting for ages and then he came. . . . He was led . . . into the room where I was." A look of pain crossed Finbar's brown face. "He was . . . I don't know words for it . . . he was *not there*. He was like somebody sleepwalking. I am not even sure he knew me."

"He was ghosted," I said.

"What's that?"

"It is when you take the spirit out of somebody so that you can control them body and soul."

"Can it be cured?"

"Yes."

There was a long silence between us. Now, instead of resenting being forced to visit Caerleon, I wanted to go, to reach Gamal and see what ailed him. How bravely he must have resisted for them to resort to such a desperate measure.

"Could you cure him?"

"Perhaps. Going there . . . trying to help him . . . might be dangerous, you know."

Finbar nodded, as if the thought of danger gave him pleasure. I was surprised to hear myself add, "It would be good to have you with me . . . someone who cares about Gamal as much as I do."

Finbar looked me in the eyes and said, "I am sorry I was rude to you that time at Euny's. I don't know why I did it. It was not the way to treat the king's daughter, and it was ungallant of me. I like you a lot, and I'd like to help you on this visit. You can trust me, and you will need people you can trust there."

He was not alone. That night, when I mentioned the visit to Erith, she said almost the same thing.

"I never liked your auntie Meroot. I don't trust that

one as far as I can see her." I sketched for her Finbar's description of Gamal.

"That poor boy!" Erith said indignantly.

IN THE DAYS that followed I made my preparations. I rehearsed spells in my head, made several flasks of clearwater, took Euny's black egg from its wrappings, and prepared herbs with a number of magic properties. I carried a little package of tidbits for Moon—Erith was disbelieving when I said that I must take the owl, but I was quite sure that I must—and of course I took my cloak and my moon amulet, which nowadays I wore all the time.

The little band that set off for Caerleon included not only Finbar but four soldiers, a bard to sing the praises of the young couple, and an astrologer-magician named Winan.

I had scant respect for the official magic of my father's court, but I thought that if I seemed to consult someone like Winan it might lull Meroot into a sense of false security about my knowledge.

So not without fear I set out for Caerleon.

The journey took us several days, but the weather was fine. At night, wrapping ourselves in our blankets, we slept under the stars. At dawn we woke to the scent of the soldiers' fire and the smell of bacon cooking. Between Finbar and me a special closeness sprang up— we were drawn together by our love for Gamal, by our sense of the dark magic that threatened all of us, and by our awareness of the dangers that might lie ahead. Our love and trust in each other, together with my largely untried magic, were nearly all the protection that we had. I insisted that Finbar use the clearwater. He laughed, but I suspected that he was glad enough of whatever protection it might afford.

Now that I had time to think about it, I was surprised at how my feelings toward Finbar had changed. The rude boy who had hurt my feelings and made me jealous was now quite different—a companion whose loyalty had been proved, whose laughter and jokes were very comforting, whose brilliant blue eyes seemed to me to see farther than most.

Even Finbar was silent, however, when we first saw the outline of Castle Caerleon against the sky. I suspect he was wondering, as I was, whether any of us would come out of it alive—or at least without the damage of spells.

I put on my cloak, which made me feel safer. As we got closer to Caerleon, we saw how grim and fortified it was, and I wondered what Gamal had felt the first time he approached it with the Gray Knight and Meroot. The guards at the gate allowed us to enter, and we rode into a courtyard where our horses were taken from us.

21

IN MY FATHER'S HOUSE the practice was for guests to be shown immediately into his presence, or if that was impossible, to be greeted by an ealdor and offered refreshment. In the Gray Knight's house, in contrast, we were left standing in the courtyard, tired and dirty. At Castle Dore you were always aware of life going on around you—you could hear chatter, laughter, and singing as people went about their work. At Castle Caerleon there was an ominous silence that grew as we waited, a silence so oppressive that our conversation fell to a whisper.

"Do you think we are being watched?" Finbar asked me quietly. I nodded. Somewhere, I knew, from the stairways and balconies above, eyes were looking coldly down upon us. I shivered.

At that moment a servant appeared and bore away all my possessions to the room I would occupy. He returned shortly to lead the soldiers to the barracks. He tried to shepherd Finbar out with the soldiers, but

Finbar stood fast, and I said firmly, "Finbar comes with me."

"My lady asked only for you," the servant said nervously.

"And I will not go without Finbar. I will explain it to your lady."

Meroot was sitting in a huge chair on a dais in the middle of a long room, which gave her the appearance of a queen awaiting her subjects. Herbs were strewn on the floor, scenting the room. The great black hound sat at her feet watching us alertly. Meroot was dressed in a silk gown of brilliant red; at her neck was a chain with flashing stones. I advanced several steps into the room, very conscious that she was studying me. She knew, I was sure, that I had the protection of my *doran*'s cloak and probably also that my skin had been bathed with clearwater. Then, as if she had only just noticed me, she rose to her feet with a small cry of simulated delight. She held out her arms to me, kissed me, and drew me to a seat beside her grand chair. It was placed lower, I noticed, on a step.

"You remember Gamal's friend Finbar," I said. Meroot gave him a bleak stare.

"I had hoped that we might speak alone," she replied.

"There is nothing that Finbar may not hear," I said. "He is my father's messenger."

Meroot hesitated and then, plainly not wishing to cross me so early in our meeting, said, "Very well."

"We were kept waiting by your servants," I said, "and we need to wash after our journey."

"Later, later," she said indifferently.

There was a pause, and again I had the unpleasant sensation of being watched. I looked around the room. Hanging tapestries might conceal a watcher. A door at the far end of the room was ajar also.

"Where is Gamal?" I asked in a loud voice. By all means, let any eavesdropper hear the conversation.

"He is unwell," Meroot said.

I stared at her. My expression showed plainly enough that I knew this statement to be a lie.

"What ails him?" I asked.

"He has a rash and a fever," she replied. "He is not well enough to see you."

"Perhaps I could help. I am trained in healing."

A look of contempt crossed Meroot's face.

"I have no doubt that you know all the old wives have to teach."

I controlled my temper, remembering the need to find a way to help Gamal.

"You know that Gamal's choice of you, Ninnoc, has brought great joy to the Gray Knight and me. As my brother's daughter, you were always dear to me, and now we shall move into a closer friendship, to which I look forward with happiness."

"And Gamal? What does he feel?"

"How can you ask? You know that he has always adored you."

"We have been friends . . ."

Her eyes flickered hypnotically. She had an oddly snakelike quality, I thought.

"You will wish to see your room. It is what we call the eastern apartment. Finbar will have a room in the barracks."

"Finbar," I said, "is part of my retinue and must have a room near me. My father was concerned about my taking so long a journey virtually alone, and I promised him that Finbar would be my bodyguard and stay always within earshot."

Meroot's eyes flickered again.

"You think yourself in danger in the Gray Knight's house?"

"There are dangers everywhere."

"When I was a girl," Meroot said icily, "such an arrangement would have caused unpleasant gossip."

"My honor and Finbar's," I said, "are beyond doubt. And I am still a child. I am surprised at you, Aunt Meroot."

Finbar had listened to this exchange with his habitual look of faint amusement, but he flashed an admiring glance at me when it became clear that I had won the argument. I was very relieved to know he would be close at hand in that sinister castle.

The two of us went with Meroot to the eastern apartment. It was large and sunlit with a big silk-hung bed. There were fine tapestries of gods and goddesses; in the one opposite the bed a goddess who seemed to be the spirit of spring was strewing flowers over a barren winter landscape. A servant had unpacked my baggage, and everything was stored neatly away. I lifted Moon out of the bag I was carrying and set him, sleepy as ever, on a beam.

I noticed a door set in one of the walls and asked for it to be opened. I sensed the servant's reluctance and thought I could detect the sound of movement in the next room. Finally Meroot nodded. The door, I saw, opened into a small, bare chamber in which there would be room to place a bed for Finbar. There was a clean patch in the dust on the floor, as if a chair had been set close to the door of my chamber and then removed. My guess was that someone had been preparing to spy.

Finally Meroot went away with her servants, leaving me alone with Finbar. We looked searchingly at each other but knew better than to speak our thoughts.

"I need to wash and rest," I said, "and so do you. But I would like to see the environs of Caerleon before dark. Later we will ride together."

Finbar nodded and went out.

When we did meet, there was something I needed to report to him immediately.

"They took the clearwater," I told him. "I questioned the servant and she swore that the flasks were not in the baggage."

"That leaves us unprotected." Finbar's face was grave. He no longer thought the clearwater a foolish notion.

"Not at all," I said. "Look." And I produced a flask from under my cloak.

"I brought one for each of us just to be sure. Use it carefully."

WITH THE REST of the retinue we attended the formal dinner that Meroot gave in welcome that night. I had taken pains with my appearance and was slightly dismayed when just before I went to the hall Moon clambered up my arm and sat firmly on my shoulder. I lifted him off gently, saying, "No, Moon," but he returned imperturbably and I knew that he meant to accompany me. I must have looked very odd when I entered the hall, but when I sat down Moon hopped on the floor and dozed off again under my chair. I sat beside the Gray Knight. He was beautifully dressed in velvet and fur and scented with a sweet rich oil. Did the scent conceal some other less pleasant odor? I suspected that it did. As I soon discovered from his conversation, the knight was well educated and had studied the astronomical wisdom of the ancients at length. He was also very courteous and I must say I was charmed by him. He had huge dark eyes that I found very attractive; every time I looked into them they reminded me of someone, though I could not think of who it was. I retired for the night more than a little under his spell.

The next morning Finbar and I were taken to see the Gray Knight's soldiers practicing on a nearby field. I was appalled by their number—they were a small army—and I knew that I was intended to be impressed by this display of might.

Three days passed. Meroot said more than once that it was a pity Gamal was too ill to meet me on this visit. There was nothing, however, to prevent us from making all the necessary plans for the wedding, though Gamal and I might not meet again until the actual day of the ceremony.

I did not know where Gamal's chamber was, closely as I watched the servants for clues, but I did know that Meroot and the Gray Knight had their private rooms in the western wing of the castle.

So it was that I formed the desperate plan of visiting

Meroot's rooms in her absence to see whether I could find Gamal or simply discover some secret about Meroot—I knew not what—that would help save him. Every afternoon, I observed, Meroot and the Gray Knight rode out together, yet I knew that her servants might be at work in her absence.

After the midday meal I pleaded a headache and a need to rest and went to my room. Later, knowing that Meroot would have left, I put on my *doran*'s cloak, and with my heart beating quite fast I went to the western wing. Meroot had a suite of rooms, and in the first of them her fat servant was asleep upon a daybed, snoring loudly. I slid silently past her into another room. This was a day room, comfortably appointed, and through an open door on the far side of it I could see Meroot's sleeping chamber. Inside there was nothing of interest except a troubling smell. Partly it was the smell of Meroot's dog—I was surprised that she allowed such a large dog in her room and also that its smell lingered even in its absence, though I was relieved that she had not left it behind to guard her quarters. Yet beyond the dog smell there was another smell that I half recognized but could not place. There was no time to think about it, however. When I opened a door on the far side of the chamber, I found myself in a workroom full of flasks and jars. A cock in a crate on the floor began to protest at the sight of me. I recognized many herbs whose uses I knew well, but everything was placed tidily on a shelf and there was nothing to indicate which jars were in use. Meroot's leather stick stood against the wall, and I picked it up and examined it with interest. It had the look and feel of a magical object, but I could not imagine what Meroot used it for.

Yet another door opened out of this room, and without much hope of finding further clues about Meroot, I opened it. For a wild moment I simply could not take in what I saw, it was so extraordinary. For there, sitting up in bed and staring straight at me, wild-eyed, was Gamal! Not only did his face show no sign of recognition of me, but he seemed unaware that any-one had come into the room. I went to the bed and took his hand.

"Gamal! It is I, Ninnoc. Do you remember?"

But as if he were deaf, blind, and without feeling, Gamal continued to stare straight ahead. I squeezed his hand, touched his white face, talked to him, but I might as well have talked to a chair. Yet I could feel that his hand trembled, see that he was sweating, smell the odor of foreboding that his body gave off. I longed to stay with him, but I knew that I could not risk it. Quietly I slid out of his room and began the journey back through Meroot's rooms toward the corridor and safety. I had gotten as far as Meroot's sleeping chamber when to my horror I heard Meroot loudly scolding her servant. I could not escape!

I was so frightened when I heard Meroot's voice coming closer that at first I could not move. Then very quickly I began to retreat toward Gamal's room. There, without thinking about it, I crawled under the bed. I was well hidden by the draperies of the bed, but I was shaking with terror at the thought of being caught. I had no idea why she had returned early from her ride, but I feared that somehow she had guessed what I had done.

She came into the room so quietly that at first I was not even sure she was there. I scarcely dared to breathe as I waited for her to lift the draperies and expose me. Then I heard her walk across the room and pour something into a goblet. She walked back to the bed, and it sounded as if she was giving Gamal a drink. There was a clink as she put the goblet down, then a long silence. After an interminable wait, Meroot to my horror said, "You can come out from under the bed, Ninnoc."

Red-faced, I crawled out, saying the first thing that came into my head.

"I thought perhaps I could help Gamal. Being a healer."

Meroot looked at me with a mixture of amused contempt and anger that made me feel not at all like a *doran* but like a very silly little girl.

"If we need your help, Ninnoc, we shall ask for it. In the meantime I shall let your father know about your appalling manners and suggest that he teach you the rudiments of what it means to be a guest. Since you have forfeited that right, I shall treat you as what you are—a naughty child. Go to your room. We shall not expect to see you at the table until tomorrow."

I went to my room fuming at Meroot's speech. Yet despite my anger I knew that there was something much more important at stake than my hurt feelings. I could not forget Gamal's staring eyes and blank white face.

22

WHEN I DID NOT appear for our evening ride, Finbar came in search of me, and it was a relief to be able to tell him what had happened. Before I spoke a word he went around the tapestries, poking them and looking behind them, and even then we spoke to each other in whispers. I could see that Finbar was impressed by my courage. I was pleased too when he decided that if I was to go without my dinner he would share my exile.

"Her anger was calculated," he said, "to distract you from what you had seen. She must be frightened now."

"The trouble is that now Meroot knows I know. What I long to do is kidnap Gamal and take him to Angharad's house. It is less than a day's ride from here. But Meroot's guards would never let him through the gate."

"Suppose we pretend that we have not noticed anything—that we believe her story about the fever. You agree to marry Gamal on the day Meroot appoints. We leave and go home. Then we return secretly and steal Gamal away. They won't know we are coming back, and he won't be guarded."

"We would never get through the gate."

"We might climb up the outside somehow," Finbar said doubtfully.

"And take Gamal out that way? In his present state?"

"What we really need is a path that leads into the heart of the house. They say that all such castles have a secret way in and out, so that if there is a siege the ealdors and their ladies can escape."

We were both silent, trying to think how, even if such a path existed, we could possibly discover it. The next day I begged Meroot's pardon, and after that I went out of my way to be nice to her, pretending to enjoy my stay and to take an interest in hawking, a hateful, bloody sport to which both she and the Gray Knight seemed addicted. I could not tell whether she was taken in—I would catch her eyes resting thoughtfully upon me, but in the days that followed Finbar and I became extraordinarily good actors. We swallowed Meroot's thinly veiled insults and the Gray Knight's cold speeches with smiles and soft words. I proclaimed that the prospect of marrying Gamal pleased me immensely, and a date was set three months hence. I let Meroot believe that though at first I had thought I was too young, my father had prevailed on me to agree, and his word was law. Perhaps I overdid it; I don't know.

Meanwhile Finbar and I spent more and more time in the countryside searching in copses and on rocky outcrops for anything that looked like a cave that might lead into a passage. Armed with candles, a tinderbox, and a makeshift lantern, we searched with ever-declining hope. On one such day—a rather hot day—we were sitting under some trees to give ourselves and our sweating horses a little shade, when I idly picked up a stick and twirled it in my fingers as we talked. Suddenly, to my great surprise, a familiar feeling ran through my hands and arms, and I felt the twig, of its own accord, move downward. As I gave an involuntary gasp, Finbar looked at my hands and saw the twig move. "It's nothing," I said, slightly embarrassed. "It may mean that water runs beneath here or that some precious stone—"

I broke off because Finbar sat up sharply, his brilliant eyes staring into mine.

"Water!" he said.

"What about it?"

"Water runs beneath the castle, does it not? There is a place in the foundations where the servants draw water from an underground stream. On my first visit, when I slept with the servants, I went there to wash myself, as we all did. The underground stream runs into the castle but it does not appear to run out again. It must stay underground for some distance; then perhaps it emerges. Could the stream lead us in?"

We were both so excited by the idea that we set off at once, riding along slowly so that we could watch the action of the twig. It took us across several fields, across a moor, and through a wood. I was just beginning to think that this was foolish—that we might follow the indications of the twig for miles—when we began to hear the gurgling noise of a stream. There, tumbling out in a waterfall from beneath a rocky outcrop, was the water we had so faithfully searched for. It gushed out so quickly that we knew it must also flow quickly underground. There would be no chance of swimming against that fast current. The only faint possibility might be of a path or tunnel, left behind perhaps from a time when the water level was higher, that we could walk or crawl along in the direction of the castle. There was no sign of such an entrance from where we stood. So together we climbed up some slippery moss-covered rocks beside the waterfall. Eventually we pulled ourselves up onto a smooth clean rock near the top. Standing there, a dizzying distance from the ground, Finbar and I both gasped. For now we could see just to the left of the waterfall a dark hole that led into the stony embankment beside the rushing water. Both of us shouted with triumph.

When we entered it we could see that the path wound back into the darkness, into a rocky tunnel. We smiled at each other and Finbar lit the candle we had brought and put it into his lantern. Picking our way with care, we began to walk along the stream in the underground tunnel, sometimes passing through rocky caverns, sometimes having to bend low to avoid bumping our heads. I felt excited and exhilarated by our discovery. If only it led to the castle!

Quite soon I noticed something that surprised me: a subdued light of a delicate greenish color came from the amulet Euny had given me. Even without a lantern it gave enough light, I thought.

Just as I was beginning to worry that the path might end anywhere, and that however interesting the tunnel we were unlikely to be helping Gamal, Finbar suddenly stopped and pointed at the upper part of the rock walls.

"What? What?" I said, unable to see anything unusual.

"It's red," he said. "The rock is red. Just like the rocks around the castle."

The path led on for another five hundred paces. Then it curved and light appeared dimly at the end of it. As we got closer to the source of the light, we could see that a great rock blocked the path but that light shone down onto the water of the stream.

"I think we have reached the castle," Finbar said, "but we will have to make sure that we can get into it from here."

The water looked dark and uninviting, and it was flowing fairly swiftly away from the castle.

"I think we could use the rock to hold on to," said Finbar. "Do you want me to see if I can do it?" It was tempting to let him try by himself, but I knew that this was my adventure just as much as Finbar's. Gamal's white face, staring eyes, and shaking hand came vividly into my mind.

"Let's stay together," I said more bravely than I felt. We waded down into the water, which was cold and deep, but I was comforted by handholds on the rock. Half walking, half swimming, we groped our way around it. Suddenly the huge bulk of the castle stood above us, and we could see two of the castle servants standing in the wash place scrubbing linen. Fortunately they were too busy working and chattering to notice our arrival. We turned and crept silently back the way we had come. We had found the way to save Gamal.

NOW WE WERE READY to make the plans for our departure. Remembering Euny's instructions, I sewed myself a belt with small pouches in it to take the protections she had given me, and I kept the moon amulet around my neck. I chatted with Meroot about the wedding and plans for the future, and still I wondered whether she believed me.

The day came for kidnapping Gamal—a perfect summer day to which I woke with a feeling of sickening fear inside me. I longed for it to be time to go, but I knew that I must appear calm and controlled, as if nothing unusual was afoot.

I said farewell to Meroot with what I prayed was convincing affection and exchanged courteous pleasantries with the Gray Knight. Our party set off on the route home—in a different direction from that of the stream.

Somehow I persuaded our retinue to leave us. Perhaps because all of us were so relieved to be away from Caerleon it was not difficult. I told them that I wished to visit my old teacher Angharad and that I would join them in two days' time. Scarcely believing our good luck, Finbar and I cantered away, soon finding the path back to the wood and the waterfall.

The worst part of that day was waiting for darkness to fall. Both of us tried to talk of other things.

"I am glad to be having this adventure with you,"

Finbar said. "I trust you." By now I trusted him too, though I was also frightened at the thought of entering the castle at its very heart. Would there be guards outside Meroot's rooms? Would any of her servants wake up? Most terrifying of all, would Meroot or the Gray Knight awaken as we passed through their bedchamber? Then would Gamal come with us, and how difficult would it be to get him to walk? Suddenly something else occurred to me, and I gasped.

"The dog, Finbar!" I said. "What about the dog?"

"I've already thought of that. There is a kennel outside in the stables, and all the dogs are kept there at night. I slept near it on my last visit and was always being woken up by their barking."

"We cannot put clearwater on before we go in case the water washes it off," I said, raising another worry. "I shall carry a flask of it for us to use when we get out of the water."

Finbar nodded, not at all sorry, I thought, to have a little magic working for him. I suspected that he was just as frightened as I was, though sometimes when we discussed the adventure, his eyes would flash with a touch of his old carefree humor.

23

I SUPPOSE WHEN we worry about things it is a way of preparing for all possible disasters in advance. What often seems to happen then is that those particular disasters never occur, but that others undreamed of do. It was like that in our rescue of Gamal.

We tethered our horses in the wood, with Moon in his bag on my saddle. Then, as before, we set off along the tunnel. It felt very different setting off on a dark night instead of on a summer afternoon, and I was glad for my belt, my *doran*'s cloak, and Euny's amulet. Soon after we entered the tunnel there was a swish of wings about our heads. We both ducked, thinking a bat was above us. To my astonishment, I saw the great white sweep of Moon's wings instead. He settled on my shoulder for the rest of the journey, clutching me hard when I slipped or stumbled, sitting on my arm when the ceiling got low. It was oddly comforting having his company.

We managed the dive, leaving Moon behind in the cave—I solemnly instructed him to wait, and he seemed to understand. Once inside the castle walls we heaved our dripping bodies onto the bank, removed our cloaks and outer garments, and anointed ourselves with clearwater. Then, with the amulet as our guide, we set off again. I could feel my heart thudding; oddly, though, I felt excited and cheerful, not terrified as I had expected.

There was no sign of a guard as we made our way to the western side. Quietly we opened the door of the antechamber, which was empty. To my relief no servants lay snoring in the outer room and no hound was in sight. On through Meroot's sinister workroom and then, much more terrifying, into Meroot's bedchamber. The two of us paused in the doorway, ready to run at any moment. If necessary, I thought, we could dash down the stairs, into the water, and back into the tunnel before they could catch us. But the only sound we heard was quiet breathing. Moonlight lit one corner of the room; the rest was in darkness. Its rays illuminated something—the turquoise collar that the hound had worn, lying on a table as if only just taken off. As I saw the collar there, a hideous smell reached my nostrils and a piercing realization came to me—what I was reminded of when the Gray Knight looked into my eyes. It was a terrible shock, but I came back to my present errand when Finbar took my hand and the two of us stole into Gamal's room. Closing the door behind us, we turned to look at Gamal, who was sitting up in bed staring in front of him, exactly as he had been on my other visit. It was terribly uncanny. Did he never sleep?

Finbar threw back the covers of the bed and, putting his arms around Gamal, half lifted him out of it. Gamal slipped down until he was crouching on the floor. Finbar and I exchanged frightened glances. But we lifted him up, each slipping an arm through one of his, and without signals or words—we felt so tuned to each other that night that there was no need of them—we began to walk toward the door. Gamal offered no resistance. On the threshold we hesitated, dreading the ordeal of walking through Meroot's bedchamber. But I took a deep breath and we set off again, the three of us walking as one, and without a glance in the direction of the bed, we passed through and into the other room as silently as we had come. By the time we got to the steps my legs had begun to shake so badly that it was quite hard to keep going, but Gamal needed more help from us there and I pulled myself together.

Finbar and I discussed at length how we would get Gamal into the tunnel. We could do nothing but push him into the water and, with one of us in front of him and one behind, ease him along as best we could. Our great fear was that not understanding what was going on, he would struggle with us—a nasty prospect in that fast-flowing water—but he did not. In fact, I had a feeling that although Gamal's mind was not with us his body was responding as well as it could. We pushed and pulled him between us onto the bank in the tunnel. I wrapped my cloak around my wet body and we set off once more along the path. To begin with I felt much safer, but gradually a hateful feeling of unease spread over me. Soon I traced it to its source—seeing the turquoise collar in the bedchamber and realizing where I had seen the look in the Gray Knight's eyes.

Just then, however, the small ancient voice of Moon began to speak in my ear.

"Run, run . . . Run fast!"

"Why, Moon?"

"He's coming! Run. Run!"

"Who's coming?"

"The dog . . . the dog . . . the dog."

I turned desperately to Finbar, who did not understand Moon's language and heard only owl noises.

"Moon says the dog is coming. We must run, Finbar!"

Finbar must have been tempted to argue with me, but he did not.

Together we tried to run, each of us holding one of Gamal's arms. But he was so inert that he slowed us to little more than a fast walk.

"We *must* run, Gamal," I said to him desperately, but I knew my words meant nothing to him. We stumbled over the slippery, sharp rocks, and more than once one of us fell, yet despite pain and the dead weight of Gamal, we dared not go slower. I was still hoping, as I am sure Finbar was, that it was all a mistake when suddenly, far behind us, I heard a terrifying bark, and a few moments later the sound of the dog panting and running and snuffling as it leaped over the rocks. A choking, evil smell reached my nose, and it came back to me— the experience of terror in the tunnel that I had known in my flying dream. With mounting horror I heard the great hound draw closer. His monstrous baying echoed like thunder in the rocky tunnel.

Even as I heard the great dog draw closer, I remembered with dismay that in our haste we had forgotten to reanoint ourselves with clearwater when we emerged from the water. What I knew now—had known ever since I saw the collar in the bedchamber—was that the dog was the Gray Knight in his magical form. In the few seconds it took me to think this I remembered in detail when Trewyn told me how she had been threatened on the road by a huge black dog who was an enemy of Angharad's in disguise. It was terrifying enough to be chased by a huge savage beast; it was much worse knowing that it had human and magical powers as well.

The three of us continued at our slow, stumbling pace—though it was clear, at least to me, that we had no hope of outrunning the dog. As the hound drew near, Finbar, in a last desperate attempt to save us, indicated a ledge above the path. Finbar leaped and scrambled onto it, and standing below, I tried desperately to push Gamal up to him while Finbar grabbed Gamal's shirt and pulled on it. The shirt tore and Gamal dropped down on me, knocking my breath out so that for a moment I was helpless.

Then, hearing Moon's little voice chant a litany of "Try again . . . try again," I seized Gamal, and with a strength that at other times would have been impossible for me, I picked him up and lifted and pushed him up toward Finbar. This time Finbar caught Gamal beneath the arms and somehow dragged him up to sit on the ledge beside him. The dog was now very near—the noise it made was deafening. I did not know how to find the strength to scramble up to the ledge—I was trembling so much. Whether Finbar managed to pull me—I remember his arms reaching down to me as my feet slipped—or whether some help reached me from my *doran* allies, I do not know. But one moment I was staring up hopelessly and the next I stood on the ledge beside Finbar. To my surprise I was suddenly much less afraid. Finbar pulled Gamal farther back on the ledge so that his legs no longer hung down, and I pulled my cloak around me and turned to confront the terror that pursued us. I noticed that my amulet now burned with a clear red light.

In the brief time before the dog reached us, when I could see its great red tongue hanging out, its eyes rolling, hear its baying cries, I reached into my pouch and took Euny's black egg in my hand. Within moments the suffocating smell of the beast seemed to surround us, so that I thought I would choke. I was aware of it crouching to spring, of its huge paw reaching up to drag me from the ledge, of its claws penetrating my cloak and piercing my leg. At that moment I threw the egg.

Later, Finbar and I had different recollections of what happened next. I thought there was a sort of flash, but Finbar said that the air seemed almost to split open; what both of us watched, unbelieving, was a beast slowly changing into a man, as the black hound became the Gray Knight. Deathly pale, he tottered on his feet, clutching his throat as if unable to breathe. He struggled like that for some moments, his face turning blue with the effort, until he collapsed on the ground, rolling to and fro in agony. Grotesquely, the front of his gray tunic was covered in egg yolk, as if I had thrown a perfectly ordinary egg at him.

I was so fascinated by the spectacle that I could do nothing but stand and watch. Finbar, however, nudged me. "Let's get away." While the Gray Knight gasped and struggled and groaned, we lowered Gamal over the edge as if he were a sack of corn, and then, still not taking our eyes off the knight, we two scrambled down. Once more the three of us set off half running, but this time there was no sound of pursuit, only the sound of Moon's wings as he glided along beside us.

24

IT WAS NOT till late afternoon that we reached Angharad's house. All day, since we had only two horses, Finbar and I had taken turns walking, and my right leg had gradually become very painful. The deep scratch, which the dog's claw had inflicted, was a livid purple, and the leg itself was beginning to swell. The terrors of the night came back to me all through the day; at such times I could not believe that we were not pursued. More than once I found myself turning around and looking over my shoulder, as if the dog were chasing us once more. Finbar too was pale and nervous and spoke little.

All this was bad enough, but at the moment when my hand went to my neck to feel the comfort of Euny's amulet, I found nothing there. I groped frantically beneath my cloak where the leather thong had been, but it was gone, and the silver moon with it. I stopped, appalled.

"It's gone. What shall I do? What *shall* I *do?*"

Finbar was kind and sympathetic, but I knew that he had no idea of the power of such a gift.

"We can't go back. There's nothing we can do, Ninnoc." I began to long passionately for Angharad's kindness and wisdom, for the comfort of her house and the pleasure of seeing her gentle face.

It was with near despair, therefore, as we breasted the hill and moved down into the valley, that I noticed that no smoke came from her smoke hole, that no wool hung drying on her storehouse walls. As we arrived at the house, I knew in my bones that it was empty—that Angharad was away on a journey. I was so disappointed that I began to cry. I thought I could not go on.

Of course, it felt good to reach the house and look once more upon the big room where I had learned to spin and weave and where Trewyn and I had worked and laughed. What was odd was that everything seemed ready for us—peats and wood piled beside the fire, fresh milk and bread as well as other food on the table, the loom itself with a shuttleful of green wool, as if at any moment Angharad might come in and take it up. That encouraged me. Angharad must mean to return soon. With a lighter spirit than I had felt all day I made one further exhausted effort. I laid and lit the fire and set about preparing a supper of porridge.

Finbar and I had not eaten for a day, and once we had dined (and painstakingly fed spoonfuls of porridge into Gamal), we both cheered up. I had taken the precaution of fastening the bolts on Angharad's doors; sitting comfortably by the fire with Gamal safe between us, everything suddenly felt much better. Finbar and I smiled at each other.

"We did it!" he said softly to me.

I climbed into my old bed and spread my *doran*'s cloak on top of me. Fingering the long tear the dog had made in it, I noticed something odd. The place in the front of the cloak where the tear began was the place where all those months ago I could not be bothered to go back to correct the mistake in the weaving.

No one will notice, I had thought, and no one had noticed. Yet it had given the dog his chance to wound me. My throbbing leg made me regret my carelessness bitterly.

I slept late the next morning—Gamal, Finbar said, never slept at all but sat staring unseeing in front of him. My leg had swollen further in the night, so that I could barely walk, and Finbar waited upon me and Gamal. Seeing my desire to keep the door bolted all the time, Finbar was reassuring.

"Meroot could not possibly know we are here, you know. Nor the Gray Knight. If he survived, which seems unlikely."

I wished I believed him. I had been trying to remember conversations between Euny and Angharad about the ability of *doran*s and sorcerers to "smell out" their enemies. My own heightened sense of smell since the *doran* ceremony made it seem only too likely that a person more experienced with magic than I might possess advanced skills of this kind. I could not recall exactly what my teachers had said, but my fear was that although it might take time, a quarry was always found in the end. My fervent hope was that Angharad would return before Meroot found us.

In the meantime we had to care for Gamal. It was unnerving having him sit with us all the time, speechless and unseeing. I loved the tender way Finbar washed his face and hands, combed his hair, tidied his clothes, and fed him. Lying weakly beside the hearth, bothered by increasing pain in my leg and full of fears and dark thoughts, I decided to distract myself by thinking about Gamal's problem and how he might be healed. I traced my way back through the long lessons in healing that Euny had led me through during our last weeks together.

"What we have to do," I told Finbar, "is find 'a path to his heart'—that's what the *doran*s say. We must think of something that matters so much to him that it will lure him out of his hiding place."

"Hiding place?" said Finbar, looking thoughtfully at Gamal. "You mean that he is in there somewhere but is too frightened to come out? I had thought that somehow he might just be . . . gone."

Certainly, looking at Gamal, he did seem to be gone. Even physically he seemed to bear less resemblance to the boy we had known. He looked wizened and faintly yellow, and when he was not completely still, he had a nervous mannerism of twitching his fingers. Occasionally a tear rolled down his cheek, which was all the more disturbing since he showed no other sign of feeling.

We sat in silence for a while, racking our brains for ideas to tempt Gamal.

"I think I know what to do," said Finbar quietly. "Music. That's what Gamal liked . . . likes . . . better than anything."

I remembered then that Trewyn had owned a rough flute, and with a bit of a search we found it. For the rest of the afternoon Finbar and I took turns picking out tunes on it. Did the music make any difference to Gamal? It was hard to be sure. His fingers moved more convulsively, and there were more tears than when we did not play, but there was no sign of the old Gamal returning. Late in the afternoon, when the pain in my leg was becoming so bad that I could no longer ignore it, I had a fleeting, shameful longing to shake Gamal, as if to force him to talk to us.

Finbar, at my request, had started dipping rags in cold water and spreading them over my badly swollen leg, alternating them with others as hot as I could bear. I began to shiver, and he put a hand on my forehead.

"You've got a fever," he said gravely. As he helped me up the ladder to my bedchamber, I suddenly looked around the big room.

"Where's Moon?" I asked. The previous night Moon had slept on his beam, but I suddenly realized that I had not seen him all day. He had never stayed away during the day before. I began to weep.

"First the amulet, now Moon," I said. I could not bear it.

Lying in bed, I could hear Finbar playing tunes to

Gamal and could picture the blank look on Gamal's face. As my pain grew worse and worse, I cried and shivered and sweated with fever. Although we had gotten Gamal away from Meroot, I felt that I had failed in my *doran*'s power. I had let the dog tear me, and the poison of the wound might easily kill me. Tossing and moaning, I knew that I had not wanted power with the "purity of spirit" of which Euny had once spoken, but in order to be superior to others. This reminded me of how hard it had been to relinquish the idea of inheriting my father's throne, of how jealous I had been of the unborn child who would supplant me. I had wanted the throne as much as I had wanted to be a famous and successful *doran*. Now it was too late to be anything at all.

As the pain grew worse, at times I seemed to be no longer in the white room but back in the dreadful tunnel with the sound of snuffling and baying pursuing me. I would be conscious for a while of the bed and my pain and then would be off once again down the dark, fearful corridors of my own mind. This torment went on, I believe, for hours. The house was quiet now—Finbar must have been asleep.

Suddenly I heard a baby cry. It was the cry of a very tiny child, a babe newborn, and it was as close as if it were in the room with me. I was so surprised that I sat up. The room shone with a blue-white light, and within it I saw the great throne in the council chamber and my father in his kingly robes sitting upon it. What I saw was power—a certain sort of power—and it was attractive to me. It could be used well, I knew, not to gratify one's own vanity or to make oneself rich, but to make a country safe and prosperous and to dispense justice. I had seen my father exercise his power in just this way. I knew I wanted it—I wanted the dignity, the respect, the sense of being the one to whom attention was paid and to whom others had to listen. I wanted my father's throne.

Just then I heard the baby's cry again, weak but piercing. Its pathos moved me deeply. As I thought of it, I could see the baby, a little naked boy child wrinkling his face as he cried, feebly moving his tiny hands. I felt an unbearable longing to comfort and protect him, to use my grown-up strength and knowledge as a safeguard until he grew big and strong. *This* was my rival, this frail, innocent thing? My mind moved unexpectedly away from the baby to Meroot. Meroot had wanted kingly power, had let her whole life be shaped into corruption by jealousy of her younger brother. She had not seen that her brother loved her, only that he had what she had not.

Questions and visions roiled in my mind. I felt myself coming to some difficult, reluctant decision. Something had to be surrendered or understood by me—I had to be different, but I did not know how. Pain, like an unwelcome visitor, lingered in the room. Sometimes I was wholly caught up in it, so that I could think of nothing else. Sometimes it withdrew a little from me, and I was desperate to escape from it. What helped somewhat was the memory of Euny and her way of dealing with hunger; she did not fight it, but accepted it calmly. I tried, not very successfully, to welcome it as if instead of being an intruder it was a favored guest.

Eventually—was it part of the delirium or not?—I thought I heard Moon's wings sweeping around the room and felt the breeze of his flight cooling my hot forehead. Soon afterward my pain eased, and I fell at last into a peaceful sleep.

It was morning when I awoke—a bright, sunny morning—and feeling weak after my fevered night, I lay motionless, conscious that the terrible pain had sunk to a mild throbbing. The sun winked on something on the floor beside the bed, and I blinked, then put out my hand, disbelieving. For there on the boards, with the broken leather thong still attached to it, was the silver amulet. Had it been caught in my clothing and fallen out when I undressed? No. I would have found it the night before. Then the memory of the sound of wings in the night came back to me, and I looked around the room. Moon sat comfortably on a beam, sound asleep. Only one explanation seemed possible. He had gone back for the amulet and brought it to me.

"I think you may have saved my life, Moon," I remarked shakily. Moon, who usually ignored my attempts to talk to him, opened his huge amber eyes, regarded me sternly for a moment, shuffled his feet, and went back to sleep.

25

MY MOTHER has had a son," I told Finbar.

"How on earth do you know that?"

"I saw it," I said. "In a kind of dream."
The swelling of my leg was gradually going down; the
pain had almost ceased. Finbar and I sat opposite each
other at Angharad's hearth with Gamal between us.

"That will mean you won't become *regulus*," Finbar
said carefully.

"I know. I saw that too. I think now that part of the
reason I am a *doran* is so I can protect the baby and
the kingdom."

"Don't you mind? It's unfair that you cannot rule
because you are a girl."

"It *is* unfair, and I *did* mind very much," I said truth-
fully. "But something has changed in me. . . ." I hesitated, trying to put difficult thoughts into words. "It
was Euny, of course. You see, I had grown up with
things—clothes and jewels, fine ponies, cups set with

precious stones, delicious food and drink . . . they were part of my father's power, a way of showing that he was rich and strong and could defeat his enemies. When I went to Euny, she had nothing—not enough food to eat, nor kindling to keep us warm—no possessions, really, at all. We just used exactly what we needed to keep alive—that and no more. We lived almost as simply as the wild creatures around us."

I caught Finbar's eye and remembered the dreadful day when I killed Borra.

"Part of Euny's power came from her simplicity. In the end I knew I'd rather have her sort of power than all my father's possessions."

"So will you end up living like Euny?"

I laughed. "I hope not. My upbringing taught me to take pleasure in many things Euny does not care about—in learning and music, in the taste of food, in keeping warm enough and well-fed enough not to be utterly miserable. But because of Euny, I don't want to live in a palace like my father, with all those precious things and an army. I don't want his sort of power. Not that his sort is wrong, but it is not what I am called to. I want something simpler where I can work out what being a *doran* means."

"Meanwhile your brother will rule at Castle Dore," Finbar reminded me.

"Probably not half as well as I would have done," I said. It annoyed me that my brother's birth automatically excluded me, even though in my heart I wanted something very different from being *regulus*. "But I will use my power in a different way."

There was silence between us, and we both looked at Gamal, wishing that my power might do something more for him. Finbar's patient work with the flute had had no effect on Gamal at all. Suddenly I had an idea.

"The tune!" I said. "There was a special tune, a rather beautiful lullaby that Gamal remembered someone singing to him when he was a little boy. I think I know how it went." Not stopping to pick out the notes on the flute, I began to sing Gamal's tune to him slowly as I fumbled to recall it, my eyes fixed on his face. When I finished, not getting it quite right, I sang it again, this time remembering it completely. Now Finbar took up the tune, and the two of us sang it together, pouring into it our love and concern for Gamal. Then I noticed a flicker of interest in Gamal's blank face. It made me exclaim with surprise, but immediately it was gone, and I decided that the next time it happened—if it did happen again—I would ignore it and carry on as if nothing had occurred.

Later that day, quite casually, Gamal put up a hand and touched his own hair. Finbar and I pretended not to notice, but nothing more happened. That evening Gamal was as lost as ever.

"All the same," Finbar pointed out, "it does make you think that someone's in there."

The next morning Gamal coughed in such an ordinary, natural way that we both turned to him, expecting him to speak. As I fed him, I thought I saw, just for an instant, a flicker of recognition in his eyes, though at once he stared in front of him as if it were not safe to acknowledge me. Again and again that day we sang his childhood song, feeling sure now that something was beginning to change inside him.

"If he has come out of his hiding place, he needs to pretend he is still there," I thought.

We were growing short of food now, and the next morning Finbar offered to go off on a foraging expedition to try to buy meal and do some fishing. It was quiet in the house without him, and it was hard work washing and feeding Gamal all by myself. I busied myself cleaning Angharad's house—it would never do if she came home and found it dirty—and I kept the door bolted most of the time.

I was scrubbing the pots one morning a week later when I heard Finbar calling me.

"Come and see what I've got, Juniper!"

I was so delighted that he had returned that I rushed to the door and unbolted it. Even as I swung the door open it came into my mind that Finbar always called me Ninnoc. There, just a short way from the house, stood Meroot, holding her leather stick.

THE TWO OF US stood and looked at each other— accomplished sorcerer and raw *doran*. I trembled. How could I fight her experience and her cruelty? Yet I knew too that I carried within me the good inheritance of all *doran*s and that this gave me a special strength.

"What do you want?" I asked weakly.

"My son!" she said. "I want Gamal."

"You ghosted him," I said boldly. "You do not deserve to have him."

"You are speaking of things you do not understand," she said. "I know you have him here, and I have come to take him home."

I was surprised to notice then that although I was frightened of Meroot, I was much more frightened that Gamal would be taken by her and destroyed.

"You know that if a sorcerer steps on a *doran*'s territory she is in the power of the other. I have power and I shall use it," I told her, trying to keep the wobble out of my voice.

For a moment she was transfixed by surprise at my apparent confidence. Then her voice rang out imperiously. "I want my son."

Just then, as the two of us stood and glared at each other, something totally unexpected happened. From inside the house came the sound of Gamal's lullaby, played with the hesitancy of someone who has not played the flute for a long time. Meroot was as startled as I was.

"What's that?" she said.

I had heard the melody many times before, played by Gamal on various instruments and hummed by Finbar and me, yet it was as if I heard it for the first time and was struck by its extraordinary power. It spoke to me of the simplest and best kind of magic, the magic of human love, the love of the woman who had taught Gamal the song, the love of Finbar and I, who had longed so much to help our friend, the love I had begun to feel for the newborn little baby at Castle Dore. Suddenly I saw the pathos of Meroot's desperate scheming life and her unreachable loneliness. She could have enjoyed the love of Gamal and instead had nearly destroyed him.

To my surprise I found tears in my eyes when I looked at her.

"It was hard for you when your brother took the throne instead of you," I said softly. But Meroot would have none of my pity.

"And what will you do when *your* brother takes the throne instead of you?" she asked tauntingly.

"You know about that?"

"If you return Gamal to me, I will help you get your father's throne."

"If my brother is the rightful king, he shall reign at Castle Dore," I said, "and I shall do everything in my power to help him. As for Gamal, he shall choose for himself whether to return with you, since you have forfeited your natural right to care for him."

Suddenly Gamal stood in the doorway beside me.

"I am not your son," he said to Meroot, "and I shall not return with you."

At this Meroot flinched as if he had struck her, but he went on.

"I have now remembered what I could not bear to remember—that when I was a small child you took me by force from the fair-haired woman who was my mother and claimed I was your child. She was a *doran* and a woman of great goodness, but you destroyed her. You had no child, but you thought you would use me to obtain King Mark's throne. You trained me as a soldier and you bullied and threatened me to try to make me fit in with your schemes. Later you let the evil knight work his spells on me. You thought it better that he should torment me than that your plans should be frustrated. But now I am free, and I will never come back with you. I am no longer your son."

The look of mingled rage and pain on Meroot's face was a dreadful sight. She threw her leather stick at me. One moment it was a stick, but the next it had hit the earth and turned into a snake, its head near me, its tongue flicking in and out of its mouth. Gamal and I stood as if turned to stone. I had neither my cloak nor clearwater to protect me, though I was wearing Euny's amulet. Now, I knew, was the moment of power, the shift in the balance of things between Meroot's magic and the magic of the *doran*s. I picked up the snake in my right hand and held it high above my head.

"The snake is now my snake," I said. "It will do as I bid it. If you do not leave at once, without Gamal and without troubling us any further, I will order it to follow you wherever you may go, anywhere upon the earth, and to bite you. If you leave now, without spells or tricks, you will go with my blessing. The choice is yours."

Meroot hesitated, her cold eyes fixed upon mine. Then, unbelievably, she turned and shuffled away. I lowered my arm and let go of the snake, which almost at once became the leather-covered stick I remembered so well from Meroot's room at Castle Dore. For a moment I stood trying to take in all that had just happened. Then full of joy I turned to embrace Gamal.

The two of us went back inside Angharad's cottage and there—how could we believe our eyes?—were

Angharad and Euny sitting by the hearth as if they had been there all along.

"You took your time in dispatching her," said Euny, "and you nearly spoiled everything with the flaw in the cloak." But her face shone with pride in me.

Angharad got up and hugged me with her old warmth. "You did well," she said.

"The black egg worked," I told Euny gratefully. "It saved our lives. I don't know what happened to the Gray Knight, though. Do you think he died?"

Euny looked rather wickedly smug.

"Oh, he lived," she replied. "But it will be a while before he troubles a *doran* again. He has been very ill since the day in the tunnel—that particular bit of magic is very effective—and even now, I suspect, he is only well enough to take little walks around his garden."

"Does that mean one day I may meet him again?" I asked nervously.

"If your life happens that way," Euny answered. "Meeting with sorcerers is part of your job. What did you imagine? But if and when it happens, you will know what to do."

THERE WAS FEASTING in Angharad's cottage that night— Finbar returned in time to join us—and I think that I have never felt happier in my life. I loved sitting be- tween the two *dorans*—I felt so beautifully *safe*. I looked at Gamal. He was thin and pale, but life had returned to his face and his limbs, and he was again the boy I had ridden with and climbed with so often.

Angharad remembered the fair-haired *doran* who had

been Gamal's mother and answered many questions about her. Euny had visited my mother, had reassured her as to my whereabouts, and had seen the strong baby boy who was born on the night of my delirium. She insisted on looking at the scar on my leg, which bore an odd resemblance to a crescent moon. She touched the scar and murmured a spell over it, explaining that like the flaw in my cloak, if I was not careful, this could be a place where in the future dangerous magic might enter.

"What will happen to me now?" I asked the two *dorans*.

"You tell us," said Angharad.

I considered.

"I want to go home first. I must see my brother and my parents. Then . . . well, they're not really going to need me, are they? I want to travel, to see strange places, to learn more . . ." I was thinking of the need to find the place I had seen in my dream, the house by the inland cliff. I had completely forgotten Meroot's plan that I should marry Gamal, but suddenly I wondered what Gamal would do and where he would go now that he had broken with Meroot.

"I am going to become a musician at last," Gamal said, catching my eye. "There is a monastery at Streaneshalch, far in the north, in Northumbria, where they are famous for their singing and the tunes they compose. I will go there and ask if I can learn from them."

Finbar grinned. The quiet life of a monastery would not appeal to him.

"I could go back to being a page at your father's court," he said, "but really what I want to do is go to sea. I'd like to become a navigator. I will travel to the coast and persuade a ship's captain to let me join his crew."

We lifted our wine cups.

"To the mending of that which is broken," said Euny.

To which Angharad replied, "And to the finding of that which is lost."

As the youngest *doran* present, I said, "It shall be so," silently promising to do the work of the *doran*s as well as I knew how.

MONICA FURLONG is the author of several note-
worthy biographies of prominent spiritual figures,
including Thomas Merton, Alan Watts, and Saint
Thérèse of Lisieux, as well as the critically
acclaimed young adult novel *Wise Child*. Ms.
Furlong lives in London.

The witching hour…

Wise Child

by Monica Furlong

Abandoned by her parents and denied by her family, Wise Child finds herself taken in by Juniper, a sorceress. Wise Child is wary at first, but she soon flourishes under Juniper's strict yet loving hand— learning reading, herbal lore, and even the beginnings of magic. However, just as Wise Child begins to feel at home with Juniper, her mother, the "black" witch Maeve, returns, offering Wise Child an escape from her laborious life with Juniper. Forced to choose between the two, Wise Child comes to discover both her true loyalties and her own budding powers. Then Maeve's evil powers, a mysterious plague, and the fears of the townsfolk combine to place Wise Child and Juniper in what may well be inescapable danger.

"Exciting, well-written fantasy."
—*Publishers Weekly*

"A mesmerizing story…rich in detail, high in excitement, and filled with unforgettable characters."
—*Booklist*

BORZOI SPRINTERS PUBLISHED BY ALFRED A. KNOPF, INC.

She's got—

THE
POWER

by Jesse Harris

At first glance popular, pretty McKenzie Gold might seem like just another teenager. But her family and close friends realize that there's more to Mack than meets the eye. Only they know about her psychic abilities—the visions, the premonitions...the Power.

Now you can join Mack and her friends in thrilling adventures that test her supernatural powers to their limits. Read them all, and decide for yourself—*is it a gift or a curse?*

First time in print!

Borzoi Sprinters published by Alfred A. Knopf, Inc.